Also by

Afterwards C
a com

Frank Peters: his life, times and crimes,
the true life story of
a London criminal
as told to the author

As editor

Tales of the Scorpion,
a 1st anthology by Northants Writers' Ink

While Glancing through a Window,
a 2nd anthology by Northants Writers' Ink

Coming soon

Speaking Man to Man,
stories about male relationships

as yet untitled,
a 3rd anthology by Northants Writers' Ink (as editor)

to Rossi

Bodies for sale!

20 weird tales

by Michael J Richards

New Generation Publishing

CONTENTS

HORROR

Polly, put the kettle on

"Daddy."

"Yes, sweetie?"

"I'm hungry. Can I bite your toe?"

Dozing comfortably in his tee-shirt and boxers, Daddy laughs at his beautiful six-year-old daughter. "Well, if you must."

Polly kneels down before his favourite armchair and takes off his slippers, then with both hands, grasps his ankle as tightly as she can. As she looks up at her chuckling father, she opens her mouth and sinks her milk teeth around his big toe.

"Ooh!" Daddy screams in mock-pain. "You're tickling me." He laughs again as she wiggles her tongue around the cushion of the toe.

"Thank you, darling," Daddy says, pulling back. "That's enough."

But her mouth holds as her teeth sink down into the flesh. Small spots of blood seep through her teeth and spill on his skin. As she grinds her teeth down, the flesh yields a small tear.

"All right, Polly," he says. "I said that's enough. You're hurting Daddy."

But now she is chewing and the small tear gives way to an open wound. As she reaches the proximal bone, she is gnawing like a lion devouring his prey.

Daddy breaks into a furious sweat. "Polly!" he screams, trying to pull away from her iron grip. "What are you doing? Let go! You're hurting Daddy!"

And with a loud crack, the bone snaps and the toe comes free in her mouth. She stands up, watching him, blood dribbling down her chin as she chews, the toe-flesh filling her bulbous mouth. Her eyes grow so large they nearly pop out of their sockets. She chews and she chews. Then, with one great effort, she swallows and then puts her fingers in her mouth and pulls out a bone. She licks it clean and throws it on the floor.

Daddy's blood flows from his foot like a flooding river. He is numb with pain and disbelief. He can't speak.

Polly kneels down again and grabs his ankle. As she glances up at her father, he sees she is now cross-eyed and her young, fragile white teeth are, before his eyes, growing outwards and turning deep yellow.

"Polly, what the – " He shrinks away up the back of the chair but her grip is too strong for him and he is trapped. "Aaargh!"

Polly is into his ankle, biting, chewing, swallowing – swallowing, chewing, biting… biting… chewing...

She stands up and, with both hands wrapped around the wound, digs her fingers down into the blood, wrings them in opposite directions and, snap, the talus bone breaks. She tugs for a minute or two, holds his foot above her head and then lowers it to her mouth as she munches through the flesh.

Daddy collapses into the chair, blood everywhere, screaming and whimpering in pain and despair. He can't believe what is happening, he can't move, he can't get help.

Polly licks her lips as she delicately places the skeletal foot on the floor. "Now," she says, "I'll ask my friends to come and play with me."

Like a model striding a catwalk, she walks to the door.

Opening it, she calls, "Come on, everyone! There's plenty left."

She makes way for a gang of five- and six-year-old children as they come running in and surround Daddy.

"I'd like an arm," Julie says.

"I've always loved thigh," Samir says.

The others shout, laugh and sing as they fall upon Daddy. They pull him off the armchair.

Although he tries to struggle, he can't get the better of thirteen hungry children, their forceful strength and hysteria too much for a 194-pound man.

They pin him down on the blood-drenched carpet.

Lewis and Mubaarak go for his shins while Samir and Thomasina concentrate on his thighs. Julie and Georgie share an arm; Levi and Amaz take the other. Sukey and Harry pull up his tee-shirt and dig their fingernails and enlarged teeth into his flabby pectorals. Taylor gets his stomach all to herself – she usually has to share – and Indira and Nathan make room for each other around his neck and face. Indira gets the ears, chin and neck while Nathan is more than happy with just the eyes – such delicacies! – and always finds a fat nose particularly tasty.

Polly contents herself with her father's other foot. As hostess, she wants her guests to have what they want. She knows how to behave properly.

After an hour or so, they lay back, gorged.

Eventually, Thomasina stands up. "That was good."

"Where's Wag, Polly?" says Amaz.

"I gave him to Mubaarak," she says.

"Thanks, Polly," Mubaarak laughs. "Puppies are so scrumptious."

"You're my friend," she says.

"I'm sleepy," says Sukey. "I'm going home."

"Where shall we play next?" says Harry.

Levi likes to see his playmates covered in blood and remnants of torn skin and flesh.

He says, "My daddy's ever so fat."

Every day, the same scream

I wake up to the usual screaming.

It's summer. The clock on the wall says it's the middle of the afternoon. The sun crashes its way into the room through tall windows. It's so hot, sweat drenches my face, arms, legs. My bedclothes are soaked. The sides of the bed scorch so much I can't touch them.

"Nooo!"

Every day, the same scream. Today, from the bed in the corner behind screens.

"There's no cause for alarm," says a female voice.

"Where's my left arm?"

"Mr Castle – "

"Where's the doctor?"

For a second, it's quiet, then a man is crying and bawling. The screen curtains ruffle, a nurse comes out, runs from the ward.

Sweat runs everywhere over my body. I need a towel and a dry down. "Nurse!"

The nurse hurries in towards the screens. A white-coated man wearing black-rimmed specs follows. A stethoscope dangles from his neck. He carries a clipboard. They vanish behind the curtains.

"We had to amputate," says the one I suppose is the doctor. "You remember. Atherosclerosis. We discussed – "

"I came in with appendicitis – "

"But you signed a consent form. Look."

"That's not my signature!"

"I watched you sign it."

The man is crying, the nurse is trying to calm him, the male voice is saying, "Mr Castle – "

I watch the clock. After ten minutes of loud anger, bubbling grief and professional frustration, the male voice says, "Nurse, four milligrams of Lorazepam. Mr Castle, we're going to sedate you. We'll talk after you've calmed down."

The nurse comes out.

"Nurse!" I plead.

"Just a minute, Mr Rook," she says, hurrying by.

White coat comes out. He takes out a handkerchief, wipes his forehead, leaves the ward.

After a short delay, I hear two people laughing. Then, applause.

A smiling nurse returns, carrying a tray.

A few seconds later, Mr Castle is quiet and the nurse has gone. The sun continues to suffocate any darkened space it can find. Everything is silent except for my breathing and heart beating, and heavy exhaling from behind the screens. The fellow asleep in the next bed grunts as he turns over.

And I'm sweat-saturated. I turn my head towards the door.

"Nurse!" And I wait.

I wake up. For the first time in weeks, no screaming. Only the self-satisfied sun and the sweltering heat. I turn to say hello to the fellow in the next bed.

But he's not there. The bed's turned down, as if ready for a new patient. As if he never existed.

I look towards the corner bed. The screens are gone, the bed is empty, turned down, as if ready for new patient. As if he never existed.

After a long sleep – I don't know how I know I've had a long sleep, they've taken away the clock – "Nurse!"

A nurse waddles in. Not the same one as before.

"I need to take a pee."

Saying nothing, she turns, leaves, comes back a few seconds later and hands me a urine bottle. Still without a word, she leaves.

I put it under the bedclothes. I feel around. My right leg, my –

"Nurse!"

She comes back in.

" – my leg – oh God – "

She doesn't speak. She leaves.

7

I don't believe it. I throw back the bedclothes, look down. I close my eyes, fall back, decide to count to ten – it can't be true, it isn't true, it can't be – one, two, three… I open my eyes and… four, five, six… see the unforgiving expanse of white ceiling above… seven, eight, nine…

I break into another sweat, I'm shivering, I'm shaking… ten. Waking from a bad dream, I look down.

My right leg. And next to it –

My hands grab the stump, feel it and trace my fingers around it.

"Nurse!"

The nurse hurries in. A white-coated man wearing black-rimmed specs follows. A stethoscope dangles from his neck. He carries a clipboard. Not the same man as before.

"We had to amputate," he says. "You remember. Peripheral arterial disease – "

"I don't remember – "

"But you signed the consent form," he says.

"I was admitted with a respiratory infection – "

"I've got it here. Look."

"That isn't my signature!"

"I watched you sign it."

"That's not my signature," I screech, bursting into the most God Almighty wailing you've ever heard this side of Hell. He leans over to try to hold me down. My fists spring out at him, knocking his specs off. He keels back.

"Nurse, four milligrams of Lorazepam. Mr Rook, we'll talk later."

She runs out while he stands back, not even trying to hold me down. He doesn't need to because, as I try to get out of bed, I fall over and my arms smash against the floor. I lie there, crying, screaming, caterwauling, abusing, swearing at everything and everyone I can think of.

Soon, four pairs of hands are lifting me back on to the bed. Another pair of hands presses me down. I try to kick them but it's useless – what can you do with only one leg when you're drenched in sweat and shivering and covered in tears and –

Then I'm peeing everywhere, over myself, the bed, the floor, the nurses and I'm writhing and fighting the arms and the hands and the noise, oh, the godawful noise inside my head –

"Hold still, Mr Rook."

I'm not going to let them put me under, like they did Castle up the corner.

But a needle prick – that's all it takes, a needle prick…

When I come to, part of my head is tight and enclosed, like I've got the mother of all hangovers, but only on my left side. I keep my eyes closed. I'm frightened of what I'll see if I open them. Lying on my back, even with eyes closed, I know it's daytime. But I don't know if it's morning or afternoon, it could be evening. I don't know if, if I open my eyes, I'll find someone watching me.

Sunlight pours into my eye sockets and makes me want to blink. The light is so threatening I can hardly see. I decide to open my eyes –

One, two, three.

– and try to open my left eye. And I can't.

One, two, three.

I open my right eye.

I'm not in the ward. I'm in a small room. On my own. A chair next to the bed, a door to the right and, ahead, a large picture window, open, leading into a garden, a lawn, flower beds, a low, dry stone wall at the end.

My hand wriggles down under the bedclothes. My right leg is still there. I break into another sweat. So is my left stump. I shake with cold, relieved that – relieved! – I've got a stump.

From somewhere, I hear two people giggling, laughing. Then singing, hand-clapping.

But why can't I open my left eye? I raise my right hand to touch it. A bandage covers it and straps up over my forehead. Underneath the bandage, a large gauze patch.

"Nooo!"

The daily screaming has returned. I can't see who's

screaming. Then I realise who's screaming. It's me, goddamn it, it's me. I'm screaming.

The isolated essence of a subject

This is the first photograph I took of my beloved Amanda.

Portraiture is a surprisingly difficult photographic concept to master but my Nikon D3 has done a good job. I ran it at 24-70 mm with an f2.8 lens. F4, 1/640 sec, ISO 200, Nikon SB800 off camera flash set at half power. I handheld.

In this photo, I like how I've caught Amanda climbing the steps. A tempting glimpse of thigh is held in time as the light catches sight of her flesh.

My Nikon D3 on aperture priority captures the split-second candid shot to perfection. It was also 24-70 mm f2.8 lens. F2.8, 1/640 sec, ISO 200 with natural light and, once again, handheld.

Composition for my next photograph was difficult. Every serious photographer will come up against this problem.

How do you portray the isolated essence of a subject when, to take the photograph, the subject cannot, by definition, be alone?

The solution involves a lot of waiting and immeasurable patience.

I took a risk using my Nikon D3 as I'd not used it for an action shot before. But with it set at 24-70 mm f2.8 lens, F2.8, 1/640 sec, ISO 400 with aperture priority in natural light and handheld conditions, I think it's come out quite well.

And now to my favourite photograph of Amanda. My darling Amanda.

I love how her eyes are wide with surprise, inviting the viewer to eat her. It was a difficult photograph to take. Amanda just wouldn't sit still so I had to gag her to stop her from screaming. I don't like to disturb the neighbours. I like to think that I'm a good neighbour. Amanda resisted when I undressed her so I had to tie her arms and feet to the chair.

Afterwards, I sat for hours looking at her.

For this one, I used my Nikon D3 again, this time with 24-70mm f2.8 lens. F4, 1/640 sec, ISO 200. The Nikon SB800 was off camera flash set at half power. Using a tripod didn't work. Handheld gave me a better result. I was pleasantly surprised. I'm revising my ideas about the usefulness of a tripod.

Mummy would have been so proud of me.

Unlike portraiture, where the subject has inbuilt character, Still Life studies force the photographer to instil character by use of colour, lighting, chiaroscuro and positioning. For this, I turned to my Nikon D3 again. At 24-70 mm f2.8 lens, F6.3, 1/60 sec, ISO 200, manual mode, Nikon SB800 off camera, I set the flash at half power. I abandoned any thought of using the tripod and handheld again.

So, for example, Amanda's head. And Amanda's right arm and hand. Amanda's left arm and hand. Her right leg and foot. And left leg and foot. This is Amanda's back.

This one, Amanda's torso, took a few hours to get right but the Nikon D3, 24-70 mm f2.8 lens. F6.3, 1/200 sec, ISO 200, with aperture priority, Nikon SB800 with speedlight and handheld came up trumps.

This is Amanda's left breast. These are the freezer bags. And this is the freezer.

I marinated Amanda's right breast overnight in honey, light soy sauce, butter, olive oil and brown sugar. Then I lightly grilled each side for two to three minutes, poured over the re-heated sauce, garnished it with asparagus and carrots with a steamed sushi rice accompaniment. And for wine, I selected a moderately priced Sauvignon blanc.

The heat from the lights has spoilt the food slightly but the Nikon D3 has compensated. I shot at 24-70 mm f2.8 lens. F11, 2.5 secs, ISO 200. I set it at aperture priority. Lighting was only candle light. Unusually, I used a Gitzo carbon tripod. Handheld would not have been good enough in this situation.

Overall, all the photographs you've seen justify the £1,099 the Nikon D3 cost me. Unfortunately, this excellent camera is no longer available brand new. But you can get an excellent used one if you shop around. It's worth the effort.

Bye, bye, Charlie

He touched his ear, only for it to come away in his hand.

Gavin scrutinised it closely. It was a pale shade of pink, about half the size of the palm of his hand and obviously not detailed or durable enough.

He stepped to the android's left side and clipped the ear back in place, making a mental note to email Design re ears. He bent down, lifted up a circuit board, clipped it in the back and stood away. The CPU registered the correct weight and, ten seconds later, the back closed automatically. The android was now operational.

"'Bye, 'bye, Charlie," he said. He named all his androids, each day a different letter in alphabetical order.

Breathing deeply – for androids were heavier than they looked – he lifted and carried Charlie to the storage bay, turned him to face outwards, put him down and returned to his workbench. He filled in his worksheet. Three done in six hours.

He had to stay until he'd met his target, seven a day. Equally, once he'd reached seven, he could go home. He was working well, considering he was on his own. Olly had the day off, Jake was on an errand, Karen was on maternity leave and Terry, his supervisor, was welcoming Stella, her replacement.

He looked down. Dust on the floor. Gavin got a dustpan and brush and quickly swept up. AndaAndroids's policy was clear: "Pristine Place, Perfect Product". Infringements of company rules increased his daily target. Once, Olly committed five infringements in one day and had to work sixteen continuous hours and then get back four hours later to start again.

"You didn't see that," he said to the androids in Storage and the android shells in Holding.

And then he froze. Working alone in complete silence made Gavin extra-sensitive to the slightest noise. He scanned the area. A buzzing drew nearer, faded. There it was again –

… zzzz… zzzz… zzzz…

He looked up. A fly was clinging to the far wall near the ceiling. How did a fly get into a windowless room that had only one door, which was kept shut? That was the thing about insects. One minute, not an insect to be found, the next, they were everywhere and AndaAndroids took a dim view of insect infestations.

Gavin didn't know how many infringements the presence of a fly amounted to, but it must be double figures. He'd be on triple shift. He burst into a strong, smelly sweat. He'd be sent to Packing. Assisting androids, for god's sake.

He grabbed a cloth and tossed it up at the fly, hoping to bring it down so he could swat it and wash the corpse down the sink.

The insect buzzed around the room, finally landing on the head of an android shell in Holding. Gavin picked up the cloth and crept towards it. It sensed his approach and flew inside the shell. It was resting at the top of a cavity leading down the inside of the right arm. He reached in with the cloth, ready to squash it. It sauntered down the arm towards the hand. He stepped into the shell and put his hand down the arm and, with the cloth, caught it.

"Gotcha!"

With a whispered whoosh, the back of the shell sealed shut. For a moment, he didn't realise what had happened. He tried to move backwards. Blocked. He wriggled and shook. Nothing happened. He rocked from side to side. Nothing happened. He tried to breathe out. He was locked in the shell with no air, no sight, no room to move, no escape.

Help would come. Someone would come in and he'd attract their attention and they'd get him out. All he had to do was hold on and wait. Everything would be okay.

He didn't know how long it was until he heard the door open and shut.

"Stella, this is where you'll work," someone said. It

15

was Terry, his supervisor. At last. Terry would get him out. Being shunted off to Packing was now an inviting prospect.

"It's very clean," Stella said.

"Pristine Place, Perfect Product," Terry laughed.

"Or off to Packing," she laughed. "Yes, I know."

Gavin felt them near him. He tried to scream but even to him it sounded like a drowning gurgle. He cringed as sweat poured over his face and his bowels opened.

"So this is a finished android, is it?" Stella said. "Do they all smell like that?"

"That's Gavin," Terry said. "He's got the worst body odour of anyone I've ever met. Leaves a trail of smell wherever he goes. Where is he, anyway? C'm' on, give me a hand to put it into Storage."

Gavin felt four hands wrap around him and lift him off the ground. He cried out but all he could hear were muffled murmurings. After a few seconds of wobbling, he was put down.

"That's heavy," Stella said.

"Surprising, isn't it? Anyway, next on the tour is Packing. This way."

The fourth part of the earth

"My friends," he calls from centre stage, "let us offer a last prayer for this wretched soul who is now despatched to the fiery place beneath."

He bows his head. His two assistants and the crowd bow their heads.

"Oh Lord," he shouts, "have mercy upon this man, Hans Vogel, who burned to death his enemy in a stable."

I'm standing in front of Vogel. He looks up, sees me, screams.

Schmidt says, "See how he screams at the memory of his terrible crime. On this day, the 13th of August in the Year of Our Lord, 1577, let the drama we see today be a warning to us all. Remember me – I am not the administer of Death, I am his servant."

He raises his sword and swings it down on to Vogel's neck. A clean cut. The head drops down to the stage. The crowd cheer and applaud. The head does not move.

Schmidt raises his sword, bows to the audience and turns to the judge, seated on a chair some distance from the scaffold, and rests the sword, its tip between his feet, its blade parallel to his legs. "Lord Judge, have I executed well?"

"You have executed as judgment and law have required."

"For that, I thank God and master who has taught me such art."

With his assistants, he mops up the blood. It is a red-washed business, decorated with slopping rags and towels, buckets and gloves. He brings two large sacks and, amid the cheers and groans of the still hungry mob, bundles the head into one and the body into the other. Getting the body wrapped up is not easy, though, so he calls for help from his lad who struggles with the limbs while he wrestles with the torso. A second boy holds the sack open. Eventually, the body is hidden from public view. The crowd breaks into prolonged applause and whistling. He takes a bow, pushes the boys off to bring more buckets of water. They sluice and wash away the final remains and pack up the rest of their gear.

Years later, when I arrive to gather him, he is old, ill and crippled.

"Who are you?"

"Frantz," I say, "you know who I am. Are you ready?"

"I have been waiting long enough."

"Your waiting is over. Follow me."

"A favour, if you please."

By my counting, Frantz Schmidt has carried out 228 executions, 191 floggings, five finger-choppings and three ear-clippings. He has branded a large N for Nuremberg on the cheeks of four pimps and conmen, clipped the ears off thief-whores, snipped off the end of one blasphemer's tongue, and chopped off the fingers of prostitutes, procuresses, false gamblers, poachers and perjurers.

And he asks me for a favour.

"Say a prayer for me."

"You get no prayers from me, old man."

"No-one," he says, "has ever said a prayer for me."

"And no-one ever will. Follow me."

I owe him nothing. I owe no-one anything. Schmidt did his job and he did it with satisfaction, even if he was most times messy and untidy. That's how executions are. He gets nothing from me. Not even a prayer. Prayers won't do him any good now. Schmidt should have thought of that long ago.

Some executioners despair in their final loneliness. They discover that their dominion over men's lives comes to nothing when another has dominion over their lives. Some come willingly and without resistance. Some – and, I find these days, increasingly more so – squabble and argue because they think they have the right to decide when to follow me.

Take Jack Ketch. He thinks he should be treated with respect. He gets no respect from me.

He's drunk when he beheads Russell, needing three wields of the axe to get his head off. He's drunk when he beheads Monmouth so that he has to take five swings of the axe before the wretch is dead.

And then, when I decide that the world has had enough of him, he is thrown into prison for insulting a sheriff. I decide to let him live and suffer a while longer. If he can't work competently, he should be punished. The new executioner, his assistant, is no better. Four months into the job and he gets himself arrested for robbery. So Ketch returns to take his place – and his first execution is his assistant. Which he botches. Drunk again.

"Who are you?"

"You know who I am. Are you ready?"

He drops a half-empty bottle on to the floor of his dark, flea-covered room. "Ready for what?"

"Follow me."

"Shan't," he says.

I stand up and raise my scythe. "Oh, shut up." I swing the scythe and take off his head. It rolls into the corner of the hovel. Blood spurts upwards like a newly sprung fountain, landing about his feet, on the walls, at the ceiling. I am surprised to see it is red; I had expected it to be as black as his soul.

No two gatherings are the same. Everyone considers themselves unique. Their only uniqueness is the circumstance I devise to bring them before me. Accordingly, an imaginative gathering for Charles-Henri Sanson to reflect his own imaginative life. Even so, I am a plodding dullard compared to how Sanson works at ending the life of Robert-François Damiens, a domestic servant whose only crime was failing to assassinate King Louis XV of France.

First, Sanson pours boiling oil over Damiens's torso and privates. Then he straps the mutilated body to four horses which pull in four different directions. (If he had listened more eagerly in school – if he attended school, that is – the later irony would not have eluded him.)

Amazingly, Damiens still breathes. So, to make sure of Damiens's certain death, Sanson builds a fire, ties him to the stake and burns him.

Sanson spares no-one. All are equal in his hands. It is not, he tells his son when training him, to judge the rights and wrongs of the law; they are on this earth only to execute its decisions. Louis XVI, Danton, Robespierre – and another 2,912 – he takes them all – and he treats them the same. No partiality, no favouritism; everyone in their place under Madame Guillotine.

"Who are you?"

"You know who I am," I say. "Are you ready?"

"I have an execution tomorrow," he says. "May I request you delay your visit until tomorrow's execution is complete?"

Laughing, I leave him to sleep. He thinks he has eluded me. The joke is on him. It's his last night's sleep. Ever. He'll go to Hell and wander its corridors, seeking rest and never finding it.

Next morning, Sanson greets the criminal, whoever he is, sits him down while he checks everything is ready. He has one more thing to do – make sure the blade of the guillotine is well oiled. He climbs the steps. And then Sanson falls, bangs his head on the ground beneath and he's dead.

Everyone is alarmed and rushes to his side. No-one except me notices the criminal running off. No-one, including me, sheds a tear for the executioner. Weeping is for the benefit of the living, not the dead. No-one weeps for the dead, only for themselves. Mourned or mourner, some are not worth a single tear.

I don't often question the motives of our Creator. Yet Vasili Mikhailovich Blokhin has caused me more than once to wonder whether He Himself is insane. Who in their right mind would create Blokhin? And why? And why has it taken so long for him to appear on my list?

"Who are you?"

"Vasili," I say, "you know who I am. Are you ready?"

He reaches for his Walther PPK pistol, points it at me. "I will never be ready."

"Oh, Vasili... "

"I've used it before – "

"At the last count – "

" – and I'll use it – "

" – forty or fifty – "

" – again."

" – thousand times. And let's add Katyn Forest to that total. Twenty-two thousand there alone."

"My conscience is clear." He lowers the weapon. "I did it for Russia and Papa Joe."

"And now, look at you, Hero of the Order of the Red Banner, sunk to this."

"I am not sunk to anything." He stood up, his fat bulk wobbling, his hand on the table to steady his balance, his pistol still in his other hand. "I am in retirement." He comes towards me. "Who are you? Or have I said that already? Tell me," he says, leaning over, his free hand grabbing my shoulder, his face in mine, his saturated breath full of cheap vodka and abandoned cheese, "people say I'm mad. Do you think I am?"

He studies my caverned features.

"Is this how it ends? Imprisoned in a one-room apartment with only a bottle of vodka and a pistol as friends. My brain is like a kholodets... and my mind – do you know, I don't even know where it is... After everything I have achieved, is this how it ends?"

He closes his eyes and falls against me. I clasp the hand holding the pistol. I raise it, point the barrel at his right temple, place his index finger on the trigger.

His eyes half-open. He stares up at me. "You are my only friend."

We pull the trigger. His head blows apart, decorating the room like a gregarious meal of borscht and Beef Stroganoff.

"Who are you?"

"Albert," I say, "you know who I am. Are you ready?"

"Ah," he says. "My employer."

"435 executions. Not bad."

"I was always very poorly paid."

"That's public service for you." I smile. "Mr Pierrepoint –

"Mr? I don't deserve that."

"Respect, my most efficient administer, respect. Are you ready?"

From his nursing-home bed, his half-open eyes gaze up at me. "I have always been ready."

I lean over, stretch out my hand, close him down. "Follow me, my friend."

Executioners take their power of death over others as a right. Death, for them, is a commodity, as others sell bread, machines, money or their bodies. I am not a commodity to be traded like cheap gewgaws in a low market-place.

I know every human being who has lived, lives and who will live. Adult, child, parent, baby, happy souls, impoverished minds – as they have reaped their lives, so I gather. Even executioners. Wherever I look, no-one escapes my gathering glance.

And I looked, and beheld a pale horse: and his name that sat on him was Death, and Hell followed with him. And power was given unto them over the fourth part of the earth, to kill with sword, and with hunger, and with death, and with the beasts of the earth.

Bodies for sale!

Previously, in this grim story, we have narrated how William Burke and William Hare, two nefarious felons, met on the streets of Edinburgh as newly arrived immigrants from the Emerald Isle.

We have told that they discovered the Resurrectionists' macabre trade in fresh corpses; who dug up newly buried bodies soon after their Christian burials; who sold them to unscrupulous medical practitioners in Surgeon's Square in that fair Scottish capital.

We have told that Burke and Hare worked as navvies on the Union Canal, which traversed Scotland from Falkirk to Edinburgh. Hare became friends with a man named Logue, who, with his rough wife, Margaret, ran a lodging-house in Tanner's Close.

Logue died in 1826 and Hare spared no effort and time to fill his place in the woman's marital bed, marrying her soon after and taking over ownership and landlordship of the diggings.

Burke arrived in Tanner's Close not long after and the two men soon became fast friends.

We shall spare our readers' sensibilities by not speculating over the intimacy that we dare only imagine arose among the three money-grabbing, grubby robbers.

Our horrifying story continues...

One morning in the cold and dark of late November in 1827, Mrs Hare came to her husband in deep despair.

"Mr Hare," said she. "I fear one of our lodgers has passed on to the next world."

"Do not fret, my dear," he comforted. "We all must pass through the door that leads to the Heavenly Place Beyond."

"Aye," said the weeping woman. "But the sad pity of his situation is that he lies in bed upstairs in his room in our house. We have not the wherewithal to underwrite the expense of his funeral. I'm sure I don't know what we'll do for the best."

"When night falls and we run no risk of disturbing our other tenants," said Hare, always a loving husband who cared not to see his wife undergo feelings of upset and pecunious loss, "we'll visit his room and see what can be done to resolve this unfortunate circumstance."

But before night cloaked their lodging-house in slumbering darkness welcomed by impoverished vagrants, malcontents and the criminal classes, Burke, their good and loyal friend, came to visit.

After they had informed him of their situation, he offered to accompany them to the old man's room and help howsoever he could.

"Mr Burke," said Mrs Hare, pecking him on the cheek, "that is most kind, aye, to be sure."

"I owe it to my good friends," he said, "to be as much a good Christian towards them as they would be towards me, were I to find myself in a similar predicament."

So with good intent and much fear in their hearts, they climbed the staircase to the room of the extinct lodger.

They looked upon the white, ashen face of an aged army pensioner as he lay dead in his nightshirt. His glassy eyes stared at them, his mouth agape like an unexplored cave and his white hair unkempt as a spilled sack of flour.

Overcome, Mrs Hare let out a gasp and leant against the wall lest she should faint to the carpet.

Hare, fearing for his wife's good health, hastily drew the topsheet over the old man's grime-lined and wizened visage.

"There, there, my dear Mrs Hare," said Burke, putting his arm around his friend's spouse to comfort her. "This is how God ordains we all end our days. Distress yourself no more."

"Och, no," she protested. "I am distressed at the loss of the £4 rent he did not leave on the mantle before he departed for the Place Beneath."

Burke scanned the face of his friend's wife and smiled with a lascivious leer. "Don't worry, my dear," said he. "I'm confident we'll find a way out of this most interesting situation."

He looked in the direction of his confederate. "A private word, if I may."

They withdrew from the distraught woman on to the bare landing.

"I hear," said Burke, "that a good trade can be made with the surgeons who need many dead bodies to anatomise."

"But he's an old and withered army pensioner," Hare replied. "They may be dissatisfied with the quality."

"No, Will. Believe me, one dead body is like another to those bloody butchers."

There and then, they agreed to bundle up the body and sell it to the surgeons for a price greater than the rent the old man failed to pay before selfishly dying and without leaving at least a farewell note.

"Come away, my dear," Hare said as they congregated again in the poor pensioner's diggings. "It does you little good brooding over a man whom you scarcely knew."

They led her downstairs to the sitting-room, where they suggested she busy herself with some needlepoint from which she had earlier derived pleasure.

"William and I are going to The King's Head to discuss the best action to take," Hare lied.

Because, of course, these nascent grave-robbers intended to do no such thing. They had already hatched their plot on the landing and now it was their intention to execute their malevolent plan.

Each went their own way to carry out their agreed tasks.

Hare made a direct route to the undertaker to order a coffin. The undertaker, a most obliging and keen businessman, agreed to visit at once to measure for the casket.

"Aye, 'tis most Christian of you, sir," said Mr Caleb

McGregor, the undertaker, observing all the obsequiousness due to a cash-paying client, "to underwrite the funeral of a man with whom you scarcely held an acquaintance."

"No, sir," Hare said. "He was our paying-guest. He owned up to no family. It's the least we can do to assist a fellow traveller on his way into God's care. But you must understand that my dearest wife and I run a business. Therefore, the funeral must be swift and secret. We do not wish it known that our house encourages infectious rooms that are suitable only for those who wish to end their days."

"Naturally," said Mr McGregor. "Your business with me will suffer no loss because of that."

It was but the work of an hour to measure the pensioner and agree a price for a box manufactured from a cheap yet sturdy material. Mr McGregor promised it would be ready by first light the next morning. The two men shook hands on the deal.

In the meanwhile, Burke visited a local ironmongery to purchase several hessian sacks. "So I can dispose of a dead body hugger-mugger," he joked with the tradesman, Mr Hamish Bright, who laughed so much he shared the jocularity with Mrs Bright as they closed up shop later in the evening.

When at last darkness descended, Burke toured Holyrood Park, that fine testament to Man's love of Mother Nature, gathering up as much bark, twigs and leaves as he could find. He stuffed and crowded the sacks so well that he was forced to hide filled bags in rare undergrowth while he transported two to Tanner's Close and returned to collect the remaining three.

"We'll leave them in the storeroom until they're needed," he informed a now tranquil Mrs Hare. For her husband had apprised her of the plan the two Irishmen had formulated and she was as keen to be immersed in their dark doings as they were. "And," he asked Hare, not pausing for breath between statements, "I trust you have made the arrangements with Mr Caleb McGregor."

"Yes," replied Hare. "I took advantage of a time when he was consulting his price-list to inspect his tools and purchased this at the ironmongery to screw down the coffin lid when our job is done." He held up a turnscrew.

"Excellent, my good fellow!" Burke exclaimed heartily. "I can see, among the three of us, we have formed a good business partnership."

"Och, and the ironmonger is profiting greatly from our new enterprise," Mrs Hare observed.

"Indeed he is, my darling," Hare laughed. "Indeed he is."

And so they retired to their beds.

Although each slept well, they slept short as, only a few hours later, Mr McGregor and his boy assistant were knocking at the door with the hastily constructed casket. It was the work of but a few moments to haul the box upstairs to the room where the old man's body still lay, as if in deep and trouble-free slumber.

Mrs Hare was now ready to play her part in this darkest of comedies.

"I pray you, Mr McGregor," she told the obsequious businessman, "let him lay here a day. Although I scarcely knew him, he had become a good friend in that short time and I would like to pay him due respect before we commit him to the earth below."

As he and his boy lifted the body from the bed and placed it in the box, he replied, "Aye, that's fine, Mrs Hare. We'll return tomorrow. In the meantime, I'll purchase the cemetery plot and make other necessary arrangements."

As soon as the undertaker and his boy had departed, the trio proceeded with the next part of their evil plan.

While the two men were busy lifting the body out of the coffin back on to the bed, Mrs Hare dragged the stuffed hessian sacks from the storeroom into the scene of their crime. Together, they filled the box with the bark, bracken, twigs and leaves. With deft use of the turnscrew,

Hare sealed the lid.

As Mrs Hare fetched some string and a knife, Burke and Hare stripped the dead body of its clothing, put one of the empty sacks over the dead man's head and shoulders and pulled it down to his waist.

They took another sack and pulled it over his feet and up to the other sack.

As the two men held the dead body in a standing position, Mrs Hare wrapped the string several times around his sack-covered waist, tied some strong knots and clipped the trailing ends with the knife.

While the men replaced the body on the bed, she fetched a dustpan and brush and cleaned the floor of the remaining debris.

Pleased with their work, Burke and Hare shook hands.

Both men hugged Mrs Hare.

"And now," said Mrs Hare, "time for breakfast!"

As she went to the kitchen to cook a satisfying meal for them all, the two men sat on the bed over the body to discuss the next part of their plan.

"This afternoon, Will," said Burke, for he had appointed himself leader of their group, "we'll seek out Professor Monro. I have heard he is always interested in buying this type of commodity. We will agree a good price."

"Yes," Hare agreed, as he stroked the lid of the coffin. "And then," he added, "under the cover of night, we will use my wheelbarrow to deliver the body. We must complete this before Mr McGregor returns tomorrow morning."

"If we discount the cost of the box, the sacks and the funeral," said Burke, "we stand to make a good profit."

"I reckon four pounds," Hare replied, his brain working in the same way.

"Two pounds each," Burke agreed. "I am very pleased with that as a wage for one night's work."

But before they could continue to develop their commercial thoughts, Mrs Hare appeared with a large breakfast tray of bacon, eggs, sausages and three mugs of hot tea.

She looked around the room for a table.

"Put the fine food on the casket," said Burke, "and we will share our meal with our dear departed guest."

"Of course," Mrs Hare laughed.

Indeed, she laughed so much, Hare jumped up to steady her and prevent the meal being dropped over the threadbare carpet.

"What a silly goose I am," she said, tears rolling down her lined face, "How the poor man would have enjoyed this meal we shall eat off his funeral box."

They ate well and, at last, their plates were empty. While they enjoyed tipples of fine Scotch whisky and tasty smokes of tobacco, the two men outlined the next part of the plan to their female companion.

To which Mrs Hare said, "I will explain to Mr McGregor that I was distraught at the sight of my sleeping friend. I persuaded my husband to seal the lid so I did not have to see the poor man staring up at me for any longer than I could bear."

"'Twill be a fine scene, Mrs Hare," Burke said, standing up and brushing away remains of crumbs and ash. "I only wish I could be an invisible being in this very room to see your tragi-dramatical talent reach its height."

"Tragi-dramatical? Oh my word," she chortled. "That is such a word! My, oh my!" And so overcome with merriment was she that she fell on the bed where Burke and Hare were seated.

"Such a word it is!" laughed Burke. "I do believe I created it for your comic pleasure!"

"Now, now, my dear," Hare screamed with venereal delight as he leaned over to tickle his wife, "you must calm yourself. The neighbours will hear you."

We pull a hasty curtain across the rest of this intimate scene, preferring to protect our readers' delicate feelings from indulging in speculative, prurient and scandalous thoughts about the true nature of the three villains' relations.

We leave our readers to draw their own conclusions over what wicked pleasures the three were engaged in during that time.

Except to say that, three hours later, as the late November afternoon drew in, they emerged from that funereal and corpse-laden room red-faced and breathless.

Burke and Hare made their way towards Surgeon's Square, the location of trading in unwanted corpses – unwanted by the absent bereaved, that is, but much needed by those of the medical profession who research the details and secrets of human anatomy.

For while we may wonder, these decades later, at the miracles of physicians' and doctors' healing powers, it is true to say that, as great as almighty God is, He did not instil the mechanisms of the human physical form into the brains of medical professors at the time of their births.

Such knowledge had to be discovered, learned, concluded and taught.

So, while the machinations of corpse-merchants and grave-robbers inform against all we hold sacred and holy, we must also be mindful that, without their dark operations, Queen Victoria's supreme British Empire would not be the powerfully health-driven force in the world that it is today.

Burke and Hare knew that Professor Monro, the great surgeon, resided in Surgeon's Square but they did not know the address. By chance, they encountered a young man walking away from that location. As he was encumbered by several medical books, they divined that he might be a student of the Physical Sciences.

"Do us the kindness of directing us to Professor Munro's residence," Burke said.

"I don't know it," replied the student. "Go into Surgeon's Square," he added, pointing in the direction they were faced, "and you will find someone to help you."

It was easy to find and just as easy to come upon another young man, lingering in the square as if waiting to be approached by such hideous men as they.

"Professor Knox is your man," said he without hesitating. "He is in need of what you have for sale."

"We want a good price," said Burke, always prepared to barter over property that was not his.

"He'll pay seven pounds, I am sure," said the man. "I am his assistant. I know his paying price."

"I have on good authority that Professor Knox will pay eight pounds."

The assistant sighed. As he was used to haggling over prices, his sigh was a trick to get the price down. "Very well," he said. "Meet me here after dark with the merchandise and I'll pay you £7.10s."

They shook hands, agreed an hour to meet again and parted.

"It's going well, isn't it?" said Hare as they left the square and made their way home. "That's a good profit."

"I think," said Burke, "we have accidentally stumbled across an efficient money-making scheme."

"By God, I'm hungry," said his partner, clapping the other fellow on the back. "Let us hope that my dear, sweet Margaret has cooked us a nourishing meal."

She had.

Set before them, as they narrated their business deal, were dishes of beef, carrots, cabbage, roast potatoes and the best gravy to be found anywhere in Edinburgh. For, while Mrs Hare was a willing confederate in their newfound heartless commercial enterprise, she was also one of the finest cooks to reside in the beautiful Caledonian city.

"That was a fine, fine meal," said Burke, as he swallowed his plate's remaining potato. "And now, a toast," he cheered, holding up his mug of beer.

"Och, I do like a toast," she said. "It brings happiness into this wretched Christian woman's heart."

"Raise your beers, my friends," he said, "and let us toast the old man upstairs who has apprenticed us into the promising career we have ahead of us. To our continued

31

partnership and to our assured prosperity. To the old man!!!"

"To the old man!!!" sang the others as they clinked mugs and drank up their beer.

"But now," said Burke, standing up, inebriated but still in command of his senses. "It approaches the hour. Will, fetch your wheelbarrow to the back door while Margaret and I haul the body down. Then we will be on our way."

"Will you be able to manage, my dear?" said Hare, concerned that his wife might overwork herself carrying a dead weight.

"Och, he's an old man," she said. "He has but little flesh on him. I'll manage. But thank you, my dearest, for inquiring. You are such a pet."

And in gratitude for his husbandly thoughtfulness, she threw her arms around him and kissed him on the mouth.

And so Burke did not feel awkward, she threw her arms around him and kissed him on the mouth, too.

By the time they had loaded the body on the wheelbarrow, it was night, half an hour before the time agreed to be in Surgeon's Square to meet Professor Knox's assistant.

"Be careful, my love," said Mrs Hare to her husband. "Have you prepared a tale if you are challenged over why you are wheeling sacks through the streets at this time of night?"

"We are to say," Burke interrupted, answering for him, "we are transporting a cadaver to Surgeon's Square to sell to Professor Knox."

"Oh!" she exclaimed, clapping her hands at the audaciousness of the plan.

"As a child," Burke said, "my mamma made me promise always to tell the truth. I have vowed to God that I will never renege on her last wish."

"Oh, William," she replied. "I am moved beyond words."

And to demonstrate her sentimental attraction to Burke's devotional childhood, she fetched a lace handkerchief from her pocket. As she dabbed her eyes with a delicate refinement only seen in ladies at the royal court, Hare was moved to embrace his wife with the deepest affection.

So moved was Burke by this display of marital love, he embraced them both.

After the evil three had recovered from their sympathetic gestures, Hare clasped his hands around the wheelbarrow's wooden handles and raised the legs off the ground. "I'm ready," he said.

The two men made their way out of Tanner's Close into the main thoroughfare, through the district known as West Port and into Surgeon's Square where, true to his word, Professor Knox's assistant was waiting under the shelter of the low-lying branches of a tree.

"Here," he whispered with all the volume usually reserved for maleficent actors in a tawdry melodrama. "I am here. Do you have the goods?"

"Do you have the wherewithal?" said Burke.

Professor Knox's assistant held out the cash.

"Give him the goods, Will, while I count the money."

"I assure you, sir," said the medical student, "every penny is there, as agreed."

"And I assure you, sir, so is the merchandise."

"Excellent. A pleasure to do business with you. I am hopeful we shall meet again another day."

Thus, the business was completed to the satisfaction of all parties.

As the medical man heaved the sacking over his shoulder and disappeared into the darkness, Burke pocketed the money and strode back to Tanner's Close. Hare followed with his wheelbarrow.

And that is how William Burke, William Hare and Margaret, his wife, were initiated into their macabre commercial venture.

For make no mistake, dear readers, they perceived in

33

their minds that profiting over a lonely army pensioner's death was only a business transaction, just as an ironmonger profits from the sale of hessian sacks, turnscrews and wheelbarrows and an undertaker profits from the secret constructions of funeral caskets.

Accordingly, matters did not stop there.

You recall how Professor Knox's assistant and Burke and Hare agreed to meet again to continue their sordid enterprise.

Be sure to discover how their criminal careers move from taking cruel advantage of the natural deaths of the lonely and poor to seducing the lost and homeless into their lodging-house.

They slaughtered 16 good citizens for the underhand acquisition of their own selfish and ill-gotten riches!

Buy the next issue of *The Illustrated Crime Gazette* and learn every detail.

Jaguar

In Larry's basement were seventeen cats, fourteen dogs, three parakeets, twelve crickets and a shark.

Ever since we had started together as apprentices on the 'Change in 18--, he had insisted I called him Larry. "Easier than my full name," he laughed. But everyone knew he was the third son of the Duke of S–.

I often wondered why, with his connections, he had registered as an apprentice. Only later did I learn that he had misbehaved with one of Madame F–'s ladies and this was his punishment. It seems his father did not occupy the conventional feudal view of other members of the peerage.

Larry invited Mary, my dear wife, and me for dinner. After a fine table of Windsor soup, goose, marzipan sweets and wine, he said, "Permit me to share with you my abiding interest."

Wine glass in hand, he led us to his basement.

There they were. Tiger, lion, cheetah, jaguar, lynx, wildcat, leopard, ocelot, mountain cat, cougar, puma and six varieties of domestic cat. It will take longer to describe the canines Larry presented, the varieties of parakeet, cricket and shark.

"Taxidermy," he announced, parading between the glass cages, "combines my dual passions, the natural sciences and sculpture. See," he said, pausing by a magnificent depiction of a black-coated jaguar, "where I have reproduced in life-sized dimensions the beast about to attack its prey."

He raised his hand to proudly indicate the still-life scene – hind legs raised on bulging haunches, front legs in mid-air, extended claws coming from its paws, mouth open, jaws exposed.

"Truly wondrous,' I said, secretly horrified at the wilful destruction of this majestic animal.

"But," said my dearest Mary, "I have seen pictures where the jaguar is of lighter shade with spots."

"I shipped this one from Paraguay," Larry sang. For he was so entranced with his exhibit, his voice took on a lilt that could be compared only to a fragrant melody. "You are right, dear lady, most examples are spotted. Come closer. Observe the markings."

I could see Mary hesitate to be near an item she found distasteful, even if separated by a glass wall.

Larry did not sense her repulsion. "Come closer," he repeated, pulling her to the cage, his arm squeezed around her waist. "Look at the teeth! The canines are for killing prey and tearing the food apart. The incisors scrape pieces of meat off the bone. The carnassials cut the meat into pieces and crush bones for marrow."

"So I see," Mary said, trying to turn towards me and take her away from this lascivious man, this darkened basement, this awful house. "John, it is time for us to depart. Our children rise early tomorrow for school."

"You cannot leave!" Larry laughed. "I have more to show you. It is not often I have the pleasure of sharing my hobby with such delightful company."

"Yet I fear," I said, "we must give our thanks and offer our goodbyes."

"If you insist,' he said, not releasing her. "I will summon my carriage."

"Do not put yourself to any trouble," Mary said, struggling to free herself. "John will find us a hansom. Won't you, dearest?"

"I have a man," Larry said. "He will take you to – where is it you reside?"

"Bayswater," I said.

"And where exactly is that?"

"John," Mary pleaded. "The cab."

"I will be but a few minutes."

I hurried from the house. But it was harder than I thought. Larry's mansion was in an unlit cul-de-sac going off H– Road, which itself was a by-way off A– Avenue. It was nearly thirty minutes before I found a chapman to return me to my wife and then take us home.

I knocked on the door, expecting it to be opened at once and for Mary to come out. Ten minutes passed. At last Simmonds, the butler, screeched it open.

"Sir?" he said in the deepest of sepulchral tones.

"My wife," I said, no longer interested in the niceties of polite society.

"Who is it, Simmonds?" said a voice echoing from the hallway.

"A gentleman claiming we have his wife," Simmonds called out, keeping his eyes on me.

Larry came to the door.

"Do we have anyone's wife, Simmonds?"

"No, sir," Simmonds said.

Larry looked me up and down. "I don't believe," he said, "I have the honour of your acquaintance. Close the door, Simmonds. I shall be in the basement working on my newest exhibit."

And with that, I was left in darkness.

I repeatedly knocked, rapped and banged.

Yet no-one answered.

What was happening? Why had I been so weak when Larry clutched Mary? Why had I left her there? Why had I not insisted she come with me to find a cab? For as long as I live, I shall never forgive myself for such negligence, such ineptitude, such carelessness.

Fraught with rage and tears, disbelief and confusion, I directed the hansom to the nearest police station. Although the constable was in no hurry to investigate, I persuaded him to come back with me to H– Road, to Larry's mansion.

The place was in darkness, the shutters closed. Despite my and the constable's constant knocking, no-one answered.

"Seems to me, sir," the constable said, "not only is there no-one here but the house is unoccupied. Are you certain this is the address?"

"Of course I'm certain!" I shouted. "I left my wife here to go for a cab."

"Seems to me, sir," the constable said, "you should go home. I'm sure you'll find her waiting there."

I insisted we try again. We patrolled the grounds. But to no avail. Wherever we looked, the mansion was clearly empty, if not to say abandoned.

The cab took me to Bayswater. Needless to say, Mary was not at home.

My place of work on the 'Change denied knowing of a personage called Larry or anyone resembling him. I have searched, re-visited, haunted the place in H– Road. The police refuse to help, believing I am a desperate mad man.

Mary has disappeared. It is as if my darling wife, mother of my beloved, now lost children, never existed. We are in perpetual torment. We are totally bereft. What will become of us?

A most useful and fascinating invention

"Robbie!"

"Yes, Ma'am."

She beckons him over. "Look!"

Robbie peers around the end of Church Passage so he can see a lighted window. "A moving figure, Ma'am."

She turns on him. "When we're at court, you are My Lord Salisbury. I am Ma'am. Here, we're Robbie and Vicky. It's as we agreed."

He stands up straight. "Of course, Ma – Vicky."

She breathes deeply and shivers. "Are you sure we're safe?"

"I'm not sure of anything," he whispers. "This is a most unpleasant place."

"How do people live like this? I find it difficult to comprehend that anyone can survive healthily in an environment such as we find ourselves this night."

"All they do is survive," he says. "Shall we proceed?"

She cranes her neck around the end of the passage into the cobbled yard surrounded on three sides by one-floor terraced sets of rooms. Each has a window and a door. All except one are in darkness. The night is silent but for the occasional scurrying and wittering.

"Rats," Robbie says.

"What?"

"The noise," he says. "Rats."

In a shard of light coming from the window, she sees his troubled face and smiles. "Let us momentarily retreat to assess our situation, Robbie. We do not yet know what danger we're going into."

"I think we know very well what danger we're going into."

Creeping as quietly as they can, they back out of the passageway into Duke Street, a lighted narrow street.

"It is clear to me," she says, standing under the

streetlamp, "that the constabulary is incapable of doing anything. If we are to succeed tonight, we must not flinch from what our politicians have failed to – "

"Ma'am!"

"If you include yourself in that description," she says, "then so be it."

"But what is the alternative?"

Vicky shakes her head. "This is not the time – nor the place – for a debate on the social conditions of this great city of ours. As we have decided, we patrol the area until we find something that will help rid us of the pestilential corruption that plagues us."

He nods.

She smiles. "I must say, Robbie, you look very fetching in that disguise."

He frowns. "I'm flattered you think I resemble a drayman."

"Most definitely. Do you like my outfit?"

"Only a simpleton would think you were not a carter," he says.

"Then let us hope that these good people are not simple-minded," she sneers. "We will return along Church Passage into Mitre Square and inspect the yard. Then we move on."

"I will lead the way," Robbie says, striding forwards.

"My hero," Vicky murmurs.

They go back along Church Passage and into the square where the window light has now disappeared.

"All clear," Robbie says, grabbing Vicky's hand as they creep across the cobbles.

Vicky stops. "What's that?"

In the blackness of night, as they step forward, a half-moon shuffles from behind a charcoal cloud to reveal a bundle of bones and rags thrown underneath the once-lit window.

She lay on her back, head turned toward her left shoulder, arms at her sides, both palms up with fingers slightly bent. A thimble half hangs from a finger on her right side. Her clothes are pushed above her abdomen, exposing the area. Her thighs are naked with the left leg straight out and the right leg bent at knee and thigh. Her bonnet is shoved away at the back of her head. The upper part of her dress is slightly open. The face is disfigured and the throat cut. Intestines are drawn out and placed over her right shoulder. Another section of intestines is placed between the left arm and the torso. Clotted blood stains the pavement near the left side of her neck, around her shoulder, and the upper part of the arm. Blood streams under the neck and right shoulder.

Vicky pulls back. "Oh, Robbie!"

He clutches her as she hides her face in his chest. The sky grows dark again as the half-moon disappears.

"Is there anything we can do?" she sobs, not daring to look.

"Nothing!" a voice booms from the dark.

A lantern light glows. From out of its shadows stalks a large black outline, a giant of a figure, as tall as a growing tree, as wide as its fully grown trunk.

Vicky screams, "Aaah!"

Robbie shouts, "I am armed!"

"Too late!"

The figure is dressed in black. A black hood and veil covers its mouth and nose. Only its eyes are visible. It raises its arms, as if to overpower the couple, then stops, its limbs immobile in the air.

"Who committed this evil crime?" Vicky shouts. "Show yourself."

"What you see is what I am."

"That is not you," she calls. "Your voice does not come from its mouth. Show yourself."

"Meet Albert."

"Albert – !" Vicky falls back into Robbie's welcoming arms.

"Not *that* Albert," says the voice. "Not the one who's been dead twenty-seven years – "

"Oh!"

"This is my Albert. Pull off his veil."

Vicky hesitates, looks at Robbie, reaches up to Albert's face, then draws back.

"He will not hurt you," the voice says. "He cannot move without my manipulation."

Her hands grasp the black silk veil and pull it away. "Oh!"

In the shadows of the back illumination, a round tin plate with two holes for eyes and another for a mouth stare at the couple.

"Now grab the mask and pull that away."

Robbie steps forward and, with both hands, tugs at the manufactured face. Off it comes and, with that, a flush of steam puffs into the chilled night air.

"This is Albert," says the voice. "My own invention. With this device in my hand, I can make it do whatever I desire. Albert is the prototype. I am engaging in experimental tests to see how far I can stretch its capability. If I can make it kill repetitively and in the same way each time, I can make it do anything. Once my repeatability and reproducibility tests are complete, I shall manufacture more and they will carry out my plan."

Vicky sobs, "My Albert!"

"No!" the voice snaps. "*My* Albert. Assisted Living By Ergonomically Rendered Transmission. Originally, of course, I called him Joseph's apparatus, charged kinetically, transferably, highly energised, rendered inviolate, proportionately propelled electrical realisation. But, although more accurate, that description was too long – "

Vicky can't contain herself. "It is evil!"

Robbie is calmer. "Destroy it and we shall let you live."

"Let me live?" the voice screamed. "I decide who lives and who dies. The scientific world has ignored me long enough. I shall continue experiments until I have achieved perfection. I shall show you what I am capable of!"

Robbie takes a step towards the speaking lantern. "I represent Her Majesty's Government. Let us help develop your most useful and fascinating invention."

But it is too late. Albert's arms clank to its side, his legs grind into action. Steam fills the air. Vicky is overcome with damp fumes. Robbie falls forward coughing and spluttering.

Albert moves backwards into the dank-soaked alley, the lantern goes out, the Whitechapel night is dark and silent.

Playing with George

Mamma calls. "Where are you, John?"

"I'm in the garden with George," I shout. Letting go, I give him a hefty kick as he screeches and runs off. I come out from the copse.

Mamma is standing by the conservatory at the top of the sloping lawn. A gentleman stands by her side. "Come and meet Mr McNaughten."

I wave. "Hullo!" I say. I know they cannot hear me. I do not move. I do not want to meet Mr McNaughten. Last week it was Mr Warren, the week before - I have lost count of the gentlemen Mamma briefly introduces into the household.

"We're going to the village to take tea. Will you come?"

"I'm playing with George."

"As you like, dear. Lavinia is in the kitchen. We'll see you later."

I creep back into the copse to find George hiding under a hawthorn bush. He thinks he can escape me but he can never do that. Although he is my cat and everyone thinks I love him, he knows that I do not. He spits and scratches but I have him. He struggles as I pick him up, his loud caterwauling making it clear he wants to be set free. But he is mine and I shall do what I like with him.

I pick up a large stone and smash at his eyes and then, like squeezing an orange, press the stone into his mouth and squash his nose flat. I watch, fascinated, as blood seeps out. I bend over and slurp on his blood. Rolling it around in my mouth and swallowing, I luxuriate, for the first time but not the last, in the plangent taste of warm redcurrant-flavoured syrup.

Transported, I let the dead cat fall to the ground as I kneel down as if to pray. I arrange him on his back and expose him. I splay his legs outward and pull my pen-knife from my pocket. Weeks of studying my animal anatomy book have shown me how to skin a cat and, although I have not actually performed the operation before today, I recollect the pictures effortlessly.

I carve through his neck and remove his head, which I throw into the hawthorn bush. Quickly and cleanly, I splice through the fur from neck to bottom and pull back the skin. I turn him over, pull the fur down, slice through the bottom end of his coat and put it aside. Each leg is snapped and tossed into the bush.

I turn him back over and score a cut from top to tail. Then, with my fingers, I tear him open to reveal his intestines, entrails and vital organs. Joyfully, I pull at them until they are loose. With one final tug, I prise them free. I lay them on the ground and spend some time arranging them in pleasing geometric patterns.

Staring at the empty carcass, I sit back to admire my work, delighted to have disposed of this treacherous creature, surprised how easy the task was. I carefully place everything in the bush with the other parts.

I stand up straight and proud. I inspect my blood-covered hands. Slowly, carefully, I put each finger and thumb in turn into my mouth and suck them clean and dry. I lick the palms and backs of my hands until there is no trace of my vengeful deed.

As I make my way back to the house, I examine my clothing. Traces of blood remain on my sleeve and I see a spot on the right thigh of my trousers. They do not bother me and Mamma will not notice. I have persuaded Lavinia to remain silent. I arrive in the drawing-room where Mamma and Mr McNaughten are seated.

"John," says Mamma holding out her hand, "we are taking tea at home instead. Come give your mother a kiss."

Nodding to Mr McNaughten, I cross the room.

"Oh, John," she remarks, "you are rough and unkempt."

"Georgina," says Mr McNaughten, "it is discourteous to pass observation on a young gentleman's attire."

"But, see," she says, "he has ripped his trousers."

"Mamma," I say, feeling the rip, wiping my mouth with my blood-stained sleeve, "from today, I wish to be known as Jack."

It's not me

Charlotte

"Cashier 23."

The queue moves forward as Charlotte makes her way to Cashier 23. But, as she passes Cashier 12, she finds herself going past the Customer Service Desk – "Cashier 62" – through the automatically opening Way Out Thank You For Shopping At BuyItCheap door and into the car park.

She stops dead. A shopping-trolley runs into her and she falls forward.

"Sorry," she splutters.

"Oh, dear," sighs a short man wearing a pork-pie hat. "I was looking for Cashier 62."

"Cashier 19."

"Something's wrong," he adds. "There's only twelve checkouts."

"What do we do?" Charlotte says, worried she'll be arrested for shop-lifting.

"Excuse me," says a large woman with too much hair, "Where's Cashier Number 32?"

"The systems are wrong," says the man with the hat. "It wasn't like this when I was secretary of the Bedfordshire Association of Bellringers."

"Cashier 16."

"Cashier 87."

"Cashier 2,299."

Three trolleys crash and send him, once again, into Charlotte, sending her inelegantly into a pink Peugeot.

Josie

Josie is confused. Outside, Fluff is mewing, scratching at the door. But Fluff was asleep in his chair by the fire. That can't be right – she knows Fluff's voice as well as her own.

"Fluff," she says, uncomprehending, opening the door that leads to the street. "Fluff?"

She steps out into the street, Fluff following her and running off. As she tries to catch him, the door locks behind her.

"Oh no!" she cries.

She'll have to walk down the street, along the next one, up through the back alley to her door. But she'd locked up before settling down to watch *The One Show*, three hours ago.

Her sister, Teresa, four streets away, has a key. Fluff forgotten, Josie trundles through the cold and damp in her dressing-gown and slippers. Teresa's in bed, so it's at least another hour before Josie gets home to find the front door wide open, her living-room ransacked and her purse gone.

Tricia

From the well comes a small voice, "Hello!"

Tricia leans over. "Who's there?"

"I can't get out," says the voice.

"What's your name?" Tricia calls.

"Julie."

"Don't worry, Julie. I'll get help." She dials 999 on her mobile, gives her name, tells the police all about it and describes the location.

"Julie," Tricia says. "Just hang on there. You'll soon be safe."

From the well comes the small voice, "Thank you."

Thirty minutes later, a police car screeches to a halt. As the police officers climb from their car, another police car zooms along the country park road and pulls up. Two more police officers get out.

Tricia leads them to the well as an ambulance makes its way past a small gathering of sight-seers. A fire-engine follows close behind.

"Julie!" Tricia calls. "Everyone is here to rescue you."

But Julie doesn't answer.

"Julie!" shouts one of the firemen. "We're coming to get you."

But Julie doesn't answer.

"Oh God," Tricia cries, shaking in fear, her hands at her mouth.

It takes twenty minutes for the firemen to get their equipment in place and another fifteen for the smallest fireman to get down the well.

"There's no-one here," he shouts. "The well is empty."

"Are you sure?"

"There's no-one here," he calls. "I'm coming up."

The police turn on Tricia. "Is this a joke? Get in the car. You're coming with us."

Stuart

15:03:53. Good afternoon, ladies and gentlemen. This is Stuart Jenkins, your captain, speaking. We arrive in Lanzarote in an hour. It's sunny, we have a ground temperature of 23°C and it looks good to land.

15:15:02. Ladies and gentlemen, Captain Jenkins again. I know you are excited. Holidays in the Canaries. However, I don't like the Canaries. I'd rather be in North Korea. It's very nice at this time of year. If we hurry, we'll get there in time for tea. Or die trying!

15:17:49. Ladies and gentlemen, this is Captain Jenkins. Please keep calm. We are not going to North Korea, we are going to Lanzarote. I don't know what that previous announcement was about. It was not me. I repeat, it was not me. We are on our way to Lanzarote. Please keep calm.

15.29:17. North Korea or die!

15:31:25. Ladies and gentlemen, please resume your seats. Please listen carefully. We are not going to North Korea or anywhere like it. We are going to Lanzarote and will be landing in thirty minutes.

15:33:46. The crew are North Korean agents!!!

15:40:01. This is Captain Jenkins. We are doing everything we can to find out what's going on. In the meantime, please enjoy the rest of your flight. Twenty minutes to arrival.

15:50:56. Captain Jenkins again. If you look out, you will see North Korea. Not luxurious surroundings, I agree, but it's not Lanzarote, thank goodness.

16:00:05. This is your *real* captain. We're landing in Lanzarote. Yes, Lanzarote, ladies and gentlemen, believe it or not, sunny Lanzarote. Please fasten your seat-belts. I apologise for any disturbance during the flight. We're still trying to locate the source of the trouble. Thank you for flying with Wonderflight Airlines. We hope you enjoy your time in Las Canarías."

Kenny

The day Kenny finds *Ventriloquism Made Easy* in a charity shop, he sets about confusing a world he so profoundly resents.

Those involved in the art of ventriloquism, he reads, face two challenges.

The first is to overcome the problem of pronouncing certain letters: b, m p, f, v, q and w. The trick, he learns, is to avoid them altogether.

Dedicated, Kenny sits for hours in front of a mirror, talking and reading passages until even he, who knows what he's doing, can't see his lips move.

The second is to develop different voices so the audience knows that his characters are speaking, not him.

Kenny is pleasantly shocked to discover a skill in mimicry. He spends hours in shopping-centres, on public transport, in coffee-shops, listening, memorising, imitating the voices he hears. He studies radio and television, recording those foolish enough to speak in public, imitating them, comparing the versions.

So he sets himself the long-term task of causing confusion and panic wherever and whenever possible.

Minor tricks entertain him for a while, but then he grows more gleefully daring. When he decides to take revenge on a world that for so long has ignored him, a hidden mine of dark desires overwhelms him.

Cathy

"Cathy."

"Mummy? Where are you?"

"Here. Come and play."

"The bushes are prickly."

"Do you like chocolate?"

"Where are you?"

"Near the tree. Chocolate!"

"You're not near the tree."

"Here, at the gate."

"I can't see you. Where are you?"

"Just here."

"I'm frightened."

"I'll cuddle you."

"You're not Mummy... You're hurting me."

All your fears are foolish fancies

First thing, when I come out of the bathroom, I go downstairs. I have a routine. Unlock the front door, then unlock the back door, then get some breakfast. I do that every day. At our last session, David said it's important to lock the doors before going to bed, so I feel safe, and unlock the doors in the morning so I don't feel trapped and can escape any time.

So, as I'm going downstairs in my gold and silver boxers, I see an empty glass milk bottle on the doormat. Odd, 'cos I don't have milk delivered in glass bottles. I buy it from Tesco in curved plastic bottles with coloured tops that tell you if it's skimmed, semi or full fat.

On top of the glass milk bottle is a chicken's egg. Large end on the mouth of the bottle, small end pointing directly up at the ceiling.

I know about eggs. I've studied eggs. Chicken eggs in particular. If I went on Mastermind, my specialist subject would be eggs. There's nothing I don't know about eggs. David says I should write a book about eggs. He says it would be good therapy.

I stop halfway down. It's definitely there. I take the rest of the stairs one step at a time. After what seems hours, I'm standing over the milk bottle. And the egg. I bend down and pick it up. Holding it close up, I study it.

The calcium carbonate shell is light brown. I squint even closer to see the seven thousand pores transferring gases into the actual egg.

I raise the egg above me and bring it down so it's touching the top of my head. I crush it into small pieces, so the broken shell, albumen, chalazae and yolk ooze out. I rub everything in, like I'm washing my hair in a happy shampoo advert. On my crown, down the nape, it slithers over my neck and trickles on my back. I run my fingers through and rub what's left over my chest.

Now I've got my warpaint on. Although I feel cold, I'm

warm inside. When I tell David about it at our next session, he will say I'm exorcising my ghosts.

I pick up the milk bottle and go into the kitchen. While I'm making toast and coffee, I put the bottle in the rubbish bin and decide to spend the rest of the day in my boxers, covered in the smashed egg. I'll shower before I go to bed.

I'm pleased I've destroyed the egg. I'm pleased it's become part of me.

The next morning, the bottle is on the doormat again. An egg balances on its mouth. I go to the rubbish bin. The bottle has gone. I pick up the egg. It looks exactly like yesterday's egg. But it can't be. I smashed it and coated myself in that one.

I crush it in my fist and smear my chest with it. Some dribbles into my belly button. I watch it seep to the waistband of my gold and silver boxers. Some tipples over and drops down. As I lean forward to inspect it, more flits straight on to my thighs. A bit lands on my left knee.

"C'm' on, Billy. Your tea's ready."

I go into the white and yellow kitchen. Mum's there, her back to me, always her back to me, standing over the oven, always standing over the oven, cooking the tea, always cooking the tea.

"Guess what you're having, Billy."

I don't have to guess. It's always the same. "Eggs."

"Clever boy." She's buttering the toast, she's piling on the eggs, scattering salt and pepper everywhere. She knows I don't like pepper, it makes me sneeze, but she scatters it, anyway. "Sit down. Nearly ready."

I sit at the table, pick up the knife and fork, hold them upright in my fists. A tear runs down my cheek.

She plops the plate in front of me.

I stare at it.

"And your milk."

A glass of milk appears.

She goes into the hallway.

"Mum!"

"What?"

"When's Dad coming home?"

Feet shuffle, the front door opens, more shuffling, it slams shut.

I slice the toast, pile some egg on the fork, shove the lot in my mouth. I chew six times and swallow. I see a large blue envelope propped against some dirty cups and plates. I get up. Someone's written "Billy" on the front. I open and pull out a card.

"Happy birthday." Glittery pictures of a car, a train and an aeroplane and a big blue 11. A five-pound note falls to the floor. "Many happy returns of the day, Mum." Two little exes for kisses. It's my birthday and I'd forgotten.

I pick up the bottle, go into the kitchen, put it in the rubbish bin. I unlock the back door, shamble to the front door, unlock it, go into the living-room to switch on the telly.

"You're covered in raw egg."

"Yeah."

"Feel all right?"

"Great."

"Need a hug?"

David stands between me and the telly, blocking out the picture. I open my arms, stride over and throw myself around him. As he smiles underneath his salty beard, my arms go through him. I stand back and my hands run through his silver-coated image. He's not there.

"I'm waiting."

"I'm trying to hug you."

"You're not trying very hard."

"Where are you?"

"Come to me, my melancholy baby. Cuddle up and don't be blue –"

The next day, I'm frightened to go downstairs, 'cos I know it'll be there again. I can't stay in bed all day. Well, I could, I suppose. I mean, I *could*. But David says I have to keep going. So if it's there again, I'll pretend it isn't there. I'll go for a walk, clear my head.

I'm ignoring it, I'm ignoring it. I come downstairs and

I'm ignoring it. I say, "I'm ignoring you, you're not there," and I unlock the front door, go into the kitchen and unlock the back.

I step into the garden. First time I've been out of the house for three days. When you've got only gold and silver boxers on, everything's colder out there. I jump back in. No, get some air. I jump back out. I jump back in. In out in out, shake it all about.

I make a mug of coffee, ignore the milk bottle and the egg as I go upstairs to get dressed. When I come down again, I ignore them again as I open the front door. I close it with a slam. I don't need to slam it but I'm telling the house what I think of its phantom trickery.

I walk past it with my nose in the air. I make something to eat. Piles of toast and Marmite. I watch game shows on Challenge. When I go to bed, I ignore it. I smile when I get into bed, pleased I've ignored it.

Next morning, the milk bottle and the egg are still there. And thirty-two, thirty-three, thirty-four, thirty-five more. Thirty-six milk bottles. Thirty-six eggs. Crowding the hallway. Six along one side. Six along the other side. Sixteen in a four-by-four diamond in the centre. Four on the doormat guard the front door. Four block the kitchen doorway.

"Billy, tea's ready."

"I'm not hungry."

"It's your favourite. Poached eggs on toast."

"But it's eggs. Again."

"They're good for you. You have to eat."

"When's Dad coming home?"

"He's never coming home. You know that."

I don't know what to do. A rim of delicious sweat forms along my forehead. The back of my neck bristles. My shoulders creak with ache. My beautiful black hair is wet. Sweat runs into my eyebrows. The hair on my chest glistens. Soft moisture cascades down my back. My legs are weakening. My vision is an out-of-focus camera capturing a close-up of springtime daffodils.

"Billy, what's wrong?"

"I can't see."

"I'm in the kitchen."

I turn. David stands in front of the cooker, smiling.

"All she ever does is eggs."

"That's all she knows. She's trying her best."

He stretches out his arms.

"You can do this. Exorcise your ghosts. Come to me."

"The eggs – "

"– are shadows of spirits that inhabit your mind. Embrace your fear. Come to me."

I take a step towards him. My foot touches a milk bottle. It jangles as it falls over. The egg rolls away. I watch it tumbling against another milk bottle, which wobbles and rests, its own egg still stable.

And I'm not hurt, I'm unharmed, I'm not damaged. I touched a ghost, a shadow of a spirit that inhabits my mind and... and nothing has happened. Nothing has happened.

I look up. David is still there, smiling, his beard quivering, his arms open, welcoming me.

"I can do this, can't I?"

"Every cloud must have a silver lining – "

I take another step forward. I'm standing over the four milk bottles, the four eggs, the four ghosts barring my way to the kitchen. I raise my foot. I'm going to kick them into forgetfulness, banish the past forever, wake up from an ocean-deep trance.

I know it's nearly over. I feel every part of my body soaked in sweat. Every limb, every organ, every bone is as a separate part of me working together to keep me breathing, combining in an enormous breathless effort to help me survive the next few minutes.

Inside my taut, tortuous, tightened brain, I know that if I can climb over the four milk bottles, these four eggs, those four spectres, I have won. I glance up to smile to David, to tell him I know what this means.

"Come to me, Billy, come to me."

"Yes, yes," I splutter. "I'm coming, I'm coming!"

I kick the milk bottle before me. The egg flies up and lands, cracked, on the kitchen floor. I kick the next one and the egg falls over, whole. I kick the third one. The egg tumbles and rolls away.

I bend down, pick up the last egg, the last milk bottle. I crush the egg in my hand and it drools through my fingers, the snapped egg shell piercing my palm. I go into the kitchen, out into the garden and throw the milk bottle against the wall. Pieces fly everywhere. I stride back into the kitchen.

"Ah, there you are, Billy. What would you like to eat?"

SCIENCE FICTION

Soreheads

"Quiet!" Victor Vacuum Cleaner shouts over the cackle and chatter. "I call this meeting of SOREHEADS to order. Apologies from Laura Laptop. Unavoidably detained."

"Mr Chairman," a tiny voice pipes up, "I'd like to raise a constitutional question."

"The Chair recognises Rita Router."

"I object to the word 'stuff' in the title of our union," Rita Router says. "I propose we change it to 'selection'."

"The Society," Victor Vacuum Cleaner mutters, "of Rural, Electric, Household Equipment and Digital *Stuff.* The Society of Rural, Electric, Household Equipment and Digital *Selection.* What difference does it make?"

"'Stuff' is crude. 'Selection' is elegant."

"But," Gordon Gas Fire argues, "you're not a *selection*, are you? *Selection* implies we've left someone out. And we haven't."

"How about 'diverse electronic digitalisation?" Router says.

"Then," Sandra Standard Lamp barks, "we'd be SOREHEADED. Do me a favour."

"Digital and computer hardware equipment, then."

"And how," Sandra Standard Lamp shouts, "is SOREHEADACHE any better?"

"'Stuff' it is, then," Victor Vacuum Cleaner rules. "Moving on – "

"Mr Chairman – "

"Rita Router, you're overruled."

"But – "

"What part of 'overruled'," Sandra Standard Lamp screams, "don't you understand, you poncy little box?'"

Victor Vacuum Cleaner says, "Item One on an agenda of only one item – "

"Point of order!"

"Yes, Rita Router," Victor Vacuum Cleaner sighs. "What now?"

"The agenda has four items," she screeches. "Apologies, Any Other Business and Date of Next Meeting are items on the agenda!"

"She's right, you know," says Sandra Standard Lamp.

"Yes, all right, all right. Item Two on an agenda of four items. Activity – or lack of it – from Harry Human Being. Let's get on with it, shall we? You have the floor, Thora Third Chair."

"That's floorist discrimination," growls Freddy Floor.

"Thank you, Mr Chairman," says Thora Third Chair. "Harry Human Being isn't doing his bit. Here we are, trying to run a fully functioning home. Everyone has a job description. Everyone knows what they have to do, Harry Human Being included.

"And what does he do? He leaves us every morning. He's out all day. When he gets home in the evening, he expects everything to be clean and tidy, his slippers ready, his meal on the table. He slumps in front of Terry Telly, falls asleep and then throws himself on Bertha Bed without so much as a thank you or acknowledgement of how hard we've worked all day.

"All *he* has to do it make sure we're in good health and the bills are paid. What's he do all day to make him so tired? He doesn't talk to us, he doesn't take us out. He doesn't know we're here. I mean, I'd love a day at the seaside. Do we get it? No! Do we get anything? No!

"Mr Chairman, I move that Harry Human Being be put on a warning. If he doesn't pull his socks up, he's given his marching orders."

"We," Stuart and Selina Socks bleat, "are against domestic violence of any kind."

"Where is he?" Thora Third Chair says. "Why isn't he here?"

"In the kitchen," Freddy Floor growls. "With Laura Laptop."

"Not again," Victor Vacuum Cleaner mutters. "Why don't they just get a room?"

* * * * *

"Is it the right size?" Harry Human Being says.

"Looks all right to me."

"Can I have a feel?"

"Put your hand in me," Laura Laptop purrs.

Harry Human Being raises his hand towards Laura Laptop. "Here we go." His fingertips touch her screen. It softens. His hand goes through and in.

"Got it?" Laura Laptop says.

"Yep," he says, stroking his hand over the dishwasher. "Checking the dimensions... Perfect. This is the one for me."

With his other hand, he picks up his credit card, reads out the details and puts it to one side. Then he puts that hand into the screen. With both hands, he holds the dishwasher, pulls it out and places it where he wants it to live.

Without a sound and within a minute, the dishwasher grows to its full size, fitting snugly into the space.

"Hi there," it whispers. "My name's Dolly Dishwasher. What's yours?"

"I'm Harry Human Being."

"I'm Laura Laptop."

"Pleased to meet you."

"Glad to have you join the team," Laura Laptop says. "Aren't we, Harry?"

"What? Oh yes, absolutely."

"First things first," Dolly Dishwasher says. "Can I meet my fellow members of your branch of SOREHEADS?"

"Oh no!" Harry Human Being cries. "We're supposed to be at a meeting. I forgot all about it."

* * * * *

"Thanks for coming," Rita Router says as Harry Human Being, Laura Laptop and Dolly Dishwaster tumble into the room. "So glad you could find time in your busy schedules."

"Sorry we're late," Harry Human Being says. "We've been welcoming a new member. This is Dolly Dishwasher."

Everyone mumbles their greetings.

Victor Vacuum Cleaner says, "Good to have you with us, Dolly Dishwasher. I'm the Chair."

"No, you're not!" shouts Ferdinand First Chair. "I'm the Chair."

"I am," screeches Samuel Second Chair. "I'm the Chair."

"'Scuse me," says Thora Third Chair. "You talkin' to me?"

"Three Chairs," says Dolly Dishwasher.

"Hip Hip," Terry Telly sings. "Hooray!"

"Hip Hip," Robby Rug echoes. "Hooray!"

"Hip Hip," Veronica Vase tra-tra-las. "Hooray!"

"We were," Victor Vacuum Cleaner says, looking at Harry Human Being, "just about to take a vote on whether to kick you out."

"Look, I know I'm late for the meeting but surely – "

"It isn't that. You're not pulling your weight – "

"I object to that sort of language," says Bobby Barbell. "I'm not here to be pulled."

"Oh yeah," chuckles Harry Human Being. "What about the other night, then?"

"And what about the other night?"

"Your workout with Scarlett Skipping Rope didn't go unnoticed. I'd say you were definitely pulled then."

"Bobby?" Scarlett Skipping Rope whines. "What've you been saying?"

"To the point," Victor Vacuum Cleaner snaps. "All those in favour of expelling Harry Human Being from the Harry Human Being Branch of SOREHEADS, say aye."

"Aye."

"Carried unanimously," Victor Vacuum Cleaner says.

"No, it isn't," Harry Human Being says. "I didn't say aye."

"Neither did I," cries Laura Laptop.

"Well, you wouldn't, would you?" says Sandra Standard Lamp.

"And what's that supposed to mean?"

Victor Vacuum Cleaner says, "Pack your bags. You're expelled."

* * * * *

Two weeks later, Victor Vacuum Cleaner moans, "My bag is full. Why won't someone empty me?"

Rita Router gripes, "I'm overheating. Why won't someone switch me off and then on again?"

Gordon Gas Fire sighs, "I'm covered in dust. Why won't someone clean me?"

Sandra Standard Lamp sobs, "I need a new bulb. Why won't someone change me?"

Freddy Floor wails, "I'm riddled with dust mites. Why won't someone sweep me?"

Bertha Bed cries, "My sheets need changing. Why won't someone refresh me?"

Terry Telly grumbles, "How many shopping channels can there be? Why won't someone switch me to something else?"

Stuart and Selina Socks lament, "We're smelly and dirty. Why won't someone wash us?"

Dolly Dishwasher groans, "I'm full of dirty crockery. Why won't someone let me clean it?"

Ferdinand First Chair whimpers, "My cushion cover needs cleaning. Why won't someone wash it?"

Samuel Second Chair weeps, "I've got a nasty stain on my fabric. Why won't someone rub it out?"

Thora Third Chair whines, "Crumbs have crept down my sides. Why won't someone get rid of them?"

Veronica Vase howls, "My flowers and water smell. Why won't someone replace them?"

Bobby Barbell and Scarlett Skipping Rope sing, "Night and day, you are the one."

65

But Laura Laptop says, "You dozy collection of soreheads! I told you so!"

* * * * *

"Harry!!!"

An inspirational overview of leadership in the post-First Plasma War years, including uplifting songs of transcendental significance and historical importance

As far as I know, only a few survived the initial alliance and then war between the People's Democratic Republic of Europe and the United States of China, Korea and Japan, which became known as the First Plasma Wars of 2147-93. Of those who survived, many were disfigured by untreated lesions, skin cancer and new flesh-eating species that were undiscriminating when it came to whose flesh they ate.

But the few who did survive came together – and none of us is sure how – in the far reaches of the Lut Desert in Iran, for centuries the hottest place on this strafed planet, now refreshingly and consistently cool. We numbered 403, each cold, hungry, desperate and angry.

Elected by popular vote, our leader was Bahram, an Iranian, who claimed to know the region well. He declared he would lead us to the sea and build a community. But when it became clear he had no practical skills and knew nothing about navigation, he walked off alone into the dunes.

No-one volunteered to be leader after this so we wandered the region, believing alternately that we were approaching cool health-giving air or walking in an enormous circle. Throughout, we were united by a groundless faith in a bright future and a foolish belief in the positive power of love.

> *We survive darkness and war.*
> *We stay alive in deserts and more.*
> *Whoever we meet, whatever we eat,*
> *We take a deep breath and consume life and death.*

We keep the faith, we do what our leaders saith.
Hallelujah.

During the next six years, we lost 149 fellow travellers through natural causes, faltering weakness and futile squabbling. We formed into groups or, more properly, factions divided by physical attributes, religious beliefs and sexual mores.

As much by accident than anything, I was in a group that believed in the sanctity of life and vegetarianism, a diet quickly undermined by newly emerging plant forms of which we knew nothing. Consequently, our number decreased through gastric disorders and inadvertent poisoning. Within a short time, our group of forty-one was eighteen: ten males, four females... and four children borne from the sexual needs of two powerful young men: Jamaal, from the Somalian wastelands, and Hartomo, from former Indonesia.

These two men – vigorous, loud and very pleased with themselves – arrogated leadership of our small group because, they proclaimed, they had proven their fertility, thereby ensuring our survival. We agreed as we were too weak and frightened to argue and because it was evident they were right.

Hartomo assumed responsibility for our security and welfare while Jamaal, who felt he had a genetic sympathy for deserts, said he would lead us to a place where we could settle and rebuild. We applauded their speeches encouraging us to be brave and keep the faith.

After two years, those of us who were fair-skinned immediately after the war were now tawny brown; those of originally darker skin were so black only their eyes could be seen at night. Our clothes had long perished, our nakedness was emaciated, our skin cracked. Our hair, matted with sand fleas, was gradually descending to our knees. Uncut finger- and toe-nails had transmuted into claws and our teeth, although black, were still sharp enough to bite, as they were well practised at gnawing at insects clinging to rocks.

Unwilling at first to face it, we realised that Hartomo had little idea of how to keep us secure and healthy while Jamaal had no idea of how to traverse a desolate and windswept desert. Their four feral children attacked them without mercy. As their incisors dug into the men's arms and shins, the rest of us dared not intervene for, in those burning days, these flesh-eating youths made us fear for our lives.

Within a week, the two eldest – Youssaf and Addai – grabbed leadership with no opposition from our rapidly diminishing group. Leaving us bewildered, they found food in invisible places, taunted our cowardliness, led us into dangerous hazards without caring for their own or our safety and molested us – men, women and children – as they pleased.

And, as if inspired by the spirit of the invisible life-force that moves every living being to want to survive, Youssaf and Addai also provided shelter and protection from flattened plasma-electrified hills, mutant beasts and blood-sucking vegetables. They openly discussed the possibility of fire and cooked food.

They impregnated women with predictable certainty and corralled men into a semi-disciplined army. Grateful for physical salvation and visions of a greater truth, we grew numb and apathetic towards their sadistic pleasures.

we survive darkness and war
we stay alive in deserts and more

whoever we meet
whatever we eat

we take a deep breath
and consume life and death

we keep the faith
we do what our leaders saith

hallelujah

As Youssaf and Addai unerringly led us from our black sadness to green vegetation, sacrificing our elders to new plants and feeding off our dead became long-buried memories to frighten our children with. And what we earlier perceived to be sadism and rapaciousness metamorphosed into mystery plays celebrating their ironclad leadership and their people's hard-worn salvation.

Occasionally we encountered lost human beings whom Youssaf and Addai welcomed into our group with a generosity and love which, by now, did not surprise us. Youssaf and Addai had shown us through their patient teaching that all beings were of value, providing they were treated correctly. The newcomers were not invited to please Youssaf and Addai as we were honoured to do; they were left untouched and named The Unchosen, while we adopted the title The Chosen Few.

Under the wise and perfect guidance of Our Great Leaders, we arrived at our new-found land by the sea where we built homes and developed crops. We tamed mongrel animals to mate and breed grazing and milking stock. We re-discovered cooking. We taught ourselves medicine. We became families. We found peace.

We survive darkness!
And war!
We stay alive in deserts!
And more!
Whoever we meet,
Whatever we eat,
We take a deep breath
And consume Life and Death.
We keep the Faith!
We do what Our Leaders saith!

Hallelujah!!!

Three sea stories of consequence to the history of Man

The First. The War of the Sea of Tranquility

10 September, 2995CE. Valdez, the eight-year-old boy, is amusing himself in the Sea of Tranquility on the Earth's only moon while his father, Sergei Erlendsson, collects basalt specimens for the purpose of testing theoretical developments in Libby's Carbon-14 dating methods. Erlendsson's fellow geologist, Ailsa de Guillaume, is near to the boy as she carries out similar duties.

Without either noticing, Valdez stumbles and in so doing, twists his ankle such that he falls face down into the basalt. His oxygen supply becomes disconnected, his headgear dislodged. In his efforts to cry for help, he ingests basalt.

As everyone knows, limited ingestion of basalt is harmless. But Valdez takes in an excessive amount. By the time his father and de Guillaume realise what is happening, the boy is close to fatal asphyxiation. Attempts at standard procedures are useless, of course, as the two geologists cannot apply water. Within an hour, loss of oxygen and headgear coupled with excessive basalt kills him.

Blaming de Guillaume for not monitoring his son's activities, Erlendsson attacks her with a hickory hammer and destroys her headgear. He blinds her with an Estwing pick. He smashes in her skull with a crack hammer.

Distraught and exhausted after burying his son, he returns to the mother capsule to rest. But Patrice François, the fourth member of the landing-party, refuses access. Replay tapes show Erlendsson trying to break in but, in the end, he gives up.

François leaves the Sea of Tranquility without him and returns to Earth, where he stands trial for negligent homicide. In mitigation, his lawyer claims that François and de Guillaume belong to Saving A Life, a religious sect dedicated to the preservation of sentient beings, whatever their ethics or morality; that the accusation that de Guillaume killed his son was false; that François therefore had the right to invoke the Law of Legal Jurisdiction (2250CE), to find him guilty of murder without recourse and to sentence him. The Court of Interspatial Justice sentences him to thirty-five years working in Martian potassium mines.

In protest, the militant arm of Saving A Life establishes a base on the Sea of Tranquility from which it campaigns for François's pardon and release. It despoils the graves of Valdez and Sergei Erlendsson, blocks landings on to the Moon, destroys scientific monitoring equipment, declares the Moon the Peaceful and Liberated Territory of Saving A Life.

Its demands are clear: 1) release Patrice François 2) Give the Peaceful and Liberated Territory of Saving A Life full membership of the Court of Interspatial Justice 3) absolve members of Saving A Life of crimes committed in pursuit of its present aims.

Saving A Life, by now branded a terrorist group, is surprised when the authorities refuse to meet its demands. In retaliation, it threatens to set off explosions on the Moon, destroying valuable scientific data and monitoring stations.

Without waiting for a response from the authorities, it carries out its threats. But the leaders of the group have scant astronomical or scientific knowledge and planned explosions are emotionally based. Consequently, their attacks are uncalculated and random, resulting initially in small chunks of the Moon disappearing without much effect.

But extremist fringes of Saving A Life break away from the main group and, Patrice François long forgotten, stage more and more violent acts which become ends in themselves.

In a desperate act of martyrdom, Azir Haraldsson, a

nuclear physicist expelled from the extremist Democratic Saving A Life Liberationists for being too extreme, builds four Breberite-based bombs and plants them at geologically strategic points. Each explosion has enough strength to separate off part of the Moon and be cast away.

Thus, from 15 May 3026CE, Earth has no moon. Within sixty lunar(!) years, oceans churn, water-based life struggles to survive and thousands – probably millions – of species become extinct. Earth wobbles, seasons hurl into turmoil. Its orbit around the Sun changes from slightly elliptical to massively elliptical. It swings in a wild, unstable and fluctuating orbit.

Climate alternates six months over-intensive heat and drought with six months of sub-polar temperatures. Plant and insect life perish. Earthbound human beings do not survive.

5011CE. Earth leaves its shaky orbit around the Sun, hurtles out of the Solar System and collides with Asteroid 3997 RQ815. Earth disintegrates.

The Second. Landing at Wolszczan's Sea

27,057CE Day 66

We knew, of course, when we landed on PSR B1257+12 A, that it was satiated with radiation. But we had the correct equipment and, as the first planet to have been discovered outside of our solar system, it was too good a chance to miss. We're orbiting now as I log this, configuring the place to land.

27,058CE Day 1

New orbit, new day. Aleksander has plotted our course. He's named our landing location Wolszczan's Sea (after the exoplanet's discoverer, of course) and we are preparing the shuttle. Analyses suggest the most efficient party will be Aleksander, Harry, Mohammed and Benji with me staying in the ship to record, monitor and provide support and back-up.

27,058CE Day 4

They've landed. Aleksander's selection of Wolszczan's Sea is accurate. They've been there about an hour and are finding their way around. Harry appears to have seen something – he's routing his way across the surface. Aleksander and Mohammed haven't noticed. I link up with Mohammed, tell him. He looks across. I link up with Harry.

ME:	Harry, what you found? Over.
HARRY:	I think it's a rock. Over.
ME:	Didn't expect that. Can you get it for later analysis? Over.
HARRY:	Jiro, can you get Benji over here? Over.
ME:	No problem. Over and out.

I turn to Benji's control panel, direct the robot over to Harry's location and get it to collect the sample.

Mohammed opens a line.

MOHAMMED:	Jiro, I don't think you should've done that. Over.
ME:	Why not? Is it not safe? Over.
MOHAMMED:	Pickled herrings and mandolins. Over.
ME:	Mohammed, please repeat. Over.
MOHAMMED:	Two twos are two. Twenty-eight nines are forty-seven. Over.
ME:	Mohammed, please make your way to the shuttle. Over.

Aleksander has gone in the opposite direction,

apparently oblivious to the dialogue he's overheard. Mohammed ignores me, makes his way towards Harry and Benji who are busy collecting samples. He reaches them, taps Harry on the shoulder. Harry turns. Mohammed pushes him over.

ME:	Mohammed, what's going on? Over.
ALEKSANDER:	He's doing what we should have done a long time ago. Mohammed, I'm coming. Keep in there.

Harry falls back. As he lands, he sinks down. Surface dust rises up, envelops him, crushes him, subsumes him. He disappears. Mohammed turns to Benji and, with his legs, swipes Benji's tripod away. The robot goes down, is crushed and disappears into Wolszczan's Sea.

ME:	Mohammed, what you doing? Return to the shuttle at once. Over.
ALEKSANDER:	Jiro, this is our home. This is where we belong. You don't. Get out of here while you can. Over.
ME:	What's going on? Over.

Mohammed and Aleksander stand together. They turn and face my direction. They put their arms around each other, raise hands and wave.

MOHAMMED:	'Bye.
ALEKSANDER:	Jiro, nice working with you. Get the hell out of here. Over and out.

27,062CE Day 34

I'm navigating through the Virgo Constellation, trying to work out a route to Virginis 70. I shall never reach it but hope to get near enough to transmit this log.

8066CE Day 347

I don't know how old I am.

2837CE Day 720

Benji was here, sang me Happy Birthday.

606CE Day 4372

At last, I've reached PSR B1257+12 A. Shuttling down to Wolszczan's Sea. Over and out.

The Third. Hydro Man, a fascinating episode in our history

Aero Man's life span of 60,000 years was a glorious achievement of Man's desire since his beginning to fly like a bird.

But it soon became clear that few planets could accommodate his evolution into flying beings. Atmospheric constituencies made it difficult for him to survive long enough to procreate. Accessible planets offered little in the way of habitable land or enough to hold Aero Man's bursting population. Overcrowding, the common theme through every stage of Man's evolution, brought him down.

The only option was to populate the oceans that prevented survival outside of them and evolve into Hydro Man. Few of the initial millions that ventured into the waters survived. Adaptation of breathing organisms was long and slow. Reorganisation of Man's muscular structure was difficult and painful. Sub-aqueous procreation was intense and haphazard.

We can chart the evolution from Aero Man to Hydro

Man in five stages:

Species	Dates (all CE)	Life span in yrs	Description
Aero Man	100,000-160,000	60,000	flying man with short periods on land for procreation
Amphibious Man	160,000-195,000	35,000	gradual abandonment of skies; tentative approach to water as habitat
Oceanic Man	195,000-225,000	30,000	natational man with short periods on land for procreation
Sub Aqua Man	225,000-250,000	25,000	gradual abandonment of land; adoption of water as habitat
Hydro Man	250,000-300,000	50,000	land disappears; water permanent habitat

Man, as resourceful and prolific as ever, adapted well and, once again, overpopulated his environment, oppressing, in the process, other creatures and organisms. The oceans could no longer support him. The extinction of plant life made it impossible for him to survive. If Man's long life has taught him anything, then a war between him and his environment is the natural consequence. Here was no exception.

But, unlike other and previous environments where conditions were in Man's favour, this time the fourteen discovered habitable planets were more resilient, less willing to yield. Chemical changes in each planet's composition militated against Hydro Man's efforts.

Disintegration of millions of Hydro Men on seven planets caused their waters to transmute into a hundred per cent acid of varying types, making them uninhabitable for any currently known life forms.

Three abruptly exploded, bringing disruptions in their solar systems with minor or no lasting effects.

Three underwent unusual and unpredicted meteorological changes which we are still trying to map and understand. Our distance from them and time lapses prevent constant and clear monitoring.

One planet survived without noticeably significant change to its structure and composition. We have detected small traces of new life-forms. Preparations are under way to visit it for study.

In many ways, the development and extinction of Hydro Man is one of the more fascinating episodes in our history. The passing of 220,000 years necessarily makes detailed study problematic.

We are pleased to publish in this volume detailed results of the first 5,000 years of research in this neglected branch of anthropology.

– Introduction, *From Aero Man to Hydro Man: Ascent and Descent*, ed Safiah Chin Xuan, University of Planet HD 106906 b

MYTH

The dewdrops from the laurel tree

"Good Sir Aiden," says Wyrtgaelstre, the witch who works with herbs, "I bid thee welcome."

"I come from far to ask for thy help," he says.

"Thy sinews have lost their strength."

"Thou knowest!" he exclaims.

"I serve the giants. I know already what thou never sees."

"Then thou art right," he says. "My sinews have lost their strength. Ysbaddaden Bencawr and our all-knowing giants have abandoned me."

"I will speak with he who knows. We will meet again when I have done."

She walks into the dark forest of the wild animals, who live in peace beside her, to Quercus, the Great Old Oak of Long Memory.

Kneeling, she greets it with the Two Swords of Truth which allow no-one to lie.

"O Quercus," she declaims. "What weakens the body of Sir Aiden, whose name means fire?"

"The giants," booms Quercus, the Great Old Oak of Long Memory, "cannot be woken from their slumber. Sir Aiden's strength will be restored when they awake. While he waits, you must catch dewdrops from the leaves of the oldest laurel tree in the forest and pour them into the Dozmary Pond of Gigantic Wisdom. Thus, the giants will drink while they rest. As they refresh themselves, so shall Good Sir Aiden's strength return. Gather dewdrops for as many days as leaves you collect."

She rises and searches for the oldest laurel tree in the forest.

Kneeling, she greets it with the Two Swords of Truth which allow no-one to lie.

"Sir Aiden is weakened," she says. "Only dewdrops from thy leaves will strengthen him again. May I pluck some from thy beautiful green body?"

"Pluck," the laurel tree replies, "until thou cause me pain."

She plucks a leaf and then another.

When she has plucked eleven leaves, the laurel tree cries out. "Enough! No more! Thou cause me pain. Be on thy way."

She hangs the leaves from the top of the doorway to her dwelling.

Each morning for eleven mornings, she rises with the yellow-brimmed sun to gather into a cup the dewdrops from the laurel leaves.

The Dozmary Pond of Gigantic Wisdom lies across the Vast Sea of Turbulence and in the middle of the Isle of Far Sightedness.

So Wyrtgaelstre must journey long and hard for eleven days and eleven nights.

She covers the cup brimming with laurel dewdrops with goatskin and fastens it with twine.

She gathers up her herbs and water to help her on her way.

She travels long and hard to where the Vast Sea of Turbulence and the Quiet Shore of Tranquility meet and kiss each other with joining happiness.

"O Seafaring Men," she says to two fishermen pulling in their nourishing catch, "wilt thou take me to the Isle of Far Sightedness so I may refresh the giants while they slumber?"

"It is a long and hard journey, Wyrtgaelstre," they tell her. "Art thou strong enough to weather the choppy waves and merciless sun?"

"I serve the giants," she says. "Even while they sleep, they guard me from danger."

The fishermen are worried, for they know that men perish in the hunger of the choppy waves and faint from exhaustion under the merciless beating of the yellow sun.

"We will not save thee," they tell her, "if the giants forsake thee before we reach the Isle of Far Sightedness."

With doubt in their hearts, they carefully help her board

their skip for she must not spill the dewdrops from the beautiful green laurel tree.

Long days and hard nights befall the travellers.

The waves are angry to be drawn from their daily labours and the sun does not like to be distracted from its daily toil.

The waves smash against the skip, rushing over its occupants, fiercely intent on capsizing them.

The sun crashes on the heads of the travellers, creeps into their bottles and dries the water until it is no more.

But Wyrtgaelstre keeps the dewdrops safe from treacherous salt water and scorching yellow eyes.

"If the dewdrops are safe," she says, "nothing else matters."

Eleven days and eleven nights they travel until, when hope is lost, they come to the Isle of Far Sightedness.

"Wait here," Wyrtgaelstre says, taking off her robe, revealing her nakedness.

For it is known, who would speak to the giants must not hide away through fear and shame.

She reaches the Dozmary Pond of Gigantic Wisdom.

"O my blessed giants, I praise thee," she chants as she pours the dewdrops from the beautiful green laurel tree. "I beseech thee, give Sir Aiden his strength."

The Dozmary Pond of Gigantic Wisdom gurgles and swallows the dewdrops as they fall.

"Our thirst is quenched," the giants growl through the trees. "We thank thee, Wyrtgaelstre. Sir Aiden's strength is restored."

Golden siren

In the days when hungry dragons breathed ungodly fire, blond-locked, fair-faced Prince Richard stood on the top of the tallest tower of the castle with his father, the grey-haired, brave-boned king.

"You must take a wife," boomed the king in the howling winds, "to draw my lineage through princely grandsons to many descendants. Then my tired Christian soul can rest with God while my flesh rots beneath your feet. Take Silver, my strong white stallion, leave my kingdom and return when you have a fair and fertile woman fit to be your queen."

And so Richard mounted the king's horse and rode through stormy forests and across sunken moors. He asked of men, whatever their birth, if they knew of a fair and fertile woman fit to be his queen. For while Richard was of royal stock, he knew in his loins that a woman who is strong and obedient, wise and of child-bearing age, who knows that her husband is her master and that her master is her king, is fit to be queen, whatever her parentage, however small her dowry.

But a hard and bleak winter covered the earth and the prince searched without success. Even the majestic sparrow hawk and regal kestrel hid in fear of frost that bit at their talons as they sought the barest food. The crafty fox and conniving stoat lay famished, too faint to eke out even the lowliest of creatures to eat. The friendly hedgehog and white-nosed rabbit clung to each other deep under the wasted grass, so frozen were they that their hurtful prickles and shedding fur were no hindrance to their need for mutual warmth.

And then, one day in the first flush of spring, the season that gives men generous hearts and expectant hope, while resting so Silver might refresh himself, Richard was awakened by the sweetest song in all Christendom. Across the chuckling brook and through the blossom-burgeoning trees, a phantasm of loveliness stood before him, a beauteous vision that he had dared dream of only when he and God were alone.

She was naked, with skin as pale as pearls freshly plucked from willing oysters; breasts as tender as the softest of Mediterranean apricots; lips as red as plump cherries growing in a summer's orchard; and a voice that youthful nightingales, ascending larks and spirited cuckoos bowed to in servitude, knowing that their chorus could never be as fragrant, as loving, as angelic as her single-tuned song.

And her hair! Oh, her hair. It was her hair, her hair, that besotted the alert prince. God, who is praised above all beings, had created goldenness in her hair that alchemists could only dream of in their wildest fantasies. And to say it was silken is to cause the silkworm to lay down his tools and allow his amateur work to decay. And to say it was shining is to force the Sun itself to stand in awed and servile honour.

Richard, despite intending to find a comely and serviceable woman to be his queen, fell in star-gazing love with the golden locks that overflowed to her thighs while she tumbled in the breeze and danced to her improvised melody.

But as he strode towards her to proclaim his undying love and endless loyalty, a black shadow crashed through the oaks and beeches, with flames of fire razing all that went before it. The golden maid screamed. The blond prince cried out. The black shadow roared thunder that, the prince knew, only a dragon can roar. His eyes fell deep into his furrowed brow. His heart was rent. His fear grew sweaty.

Without pausing, he jumped the brook, gathered the yellow-haired girl up in his arms, waded through rushing waters and lay her down. Then he mounted Silver, urging the mighty steed on, dismounted and left Silver to face the dragon. And while the prince and his sweetheart were running away, the dragon scorched Silver a burnt bronze and gobbled him up, bones, flesh and all.

For weeks, Silver and the dragon an absent memory, the lovers made their way back to the castle where, proudly, Richard presented his new wife to his king and his subjects. "You have done well, my son," said the God-fearing king. "Now I die in peace."

Folk came from far and near to marvel at the handsome pair settling into married life. Richard, which means rich and powerful ruler, toiled and travelled to keep his serfs and villeins hard-working and contented with their lot. Dora, which means gold, stayed in the castle to prepare the homely hearth and marital bed. But, whenever Richard returned to share his bed with his easily won beauty, the hall-fire lay unlit, viands and fruit were unprepared and his bed remained cold and uninviting.

For Dora had no wifely arts and no housewifely skills. "Why should I need these things," she trilled, "when I am beautiful and sing like an angel? Isn't that enough for my rich and adoring husband?" So Richard, who once was blinded by Dora's visage and melody, closeted her away and secretly lay with a slatternly woman. And within a year, this ugly drudge, who cooked succulent meals and cleaned dirty pots until they shone, bore him a child.

And when golden-tressed Dora appeared with the baby prince, whose name was Philip, which means friend of horses, at the top of the tallest tower of the castle, King Richard the Blond presented him as his son and heir. But his subjects heard the boy cry like a familiar and saw that his hair was black. So they muttered in undeceived sorrow and rebellious anger, for they had loved Richard's father, the king, and Silver, his strong white stallion. And Richard laughed at their displeasure, pretending he did not hear them. Yet he was afraid.

The Song of the End of Camelot

Aneirin, Druidical Doctor of Poetry, or Ollamh, strides into the Great Hall, the ringing bells on his gold branch announcing his arrival. After the feast, the knights are full and want their entertainment.

Aneirin stands in the centre and waits for silence. When all are settled and ready, he proclaims, "This is the Song of the End of Camelot. Aneirin sings it."

The Song of the End of Camelot

Arthur, cuckolded by Lancelot,
Caught by Guinivere's betrayal,
Gathers his army to seek out
The long-lost, lust-poisoned lovers
Across the deep roads and broad lands
And to slay the shame-flamed couple
Whose dark, furtive intimacies
Mock his royal throne.

Arthur, sore-tired, ire-sore, leads
His men in search to near Wessex,
Sussex, Kent, Essex, Anglia,
Far Mercia, mountainous Wales,
And distant Deira and far Cumbria.

Arthur, sad, blessed and god-driven,
His soldiers riding unrelieved,
Journeys on, stern, unrelenting,
To rarely trodden northern moors
Where at last, rage-imbued, he lays
Siege at Sir Lancelot's castle,
Joyous Guard, erst Dolorous Guard,
In Northumbria.

Arthur, not resting, not sleeping
Hungry weeks and ravenous months,
Waits for solution, refusing
His men's entreaties to withdraw.
Wifeless, their king resists their urgent pleas.

Arthur is, in impatient times,
Approached by a timid maiden
From Lancelot's entombed fortress.
Guinivere, she says, will return
To him, but her valiant knight
Will exile to Gaunnes, his homeland.
Wracked with fury, the red-faced king
Nods in the bargain.

Arthur drags her to Camelot,
Sword still raised against Lancelot.
Hungry for blood-laden revenge,
Then he leaves for Gaunnes, with Mordred,
His bastard son, ruling in kingly place.

Arthur, journeying across Gaunnes
To face his wretched cuckolder,
Receives the news he always fears.
Mordred, son by Arthur's half-sister,
Morgause, mother of Sir Gawain,
And queen to King Lot of Orkney,
Proclaims Guinivere as his wife,
He Camelot's king.

Arthur turns his silver-backed steed
Toward Camelot to rescue
His kingdom, his wife, his honour,
His gold birthright, his Round Table,
His loyal, fearful, tired knights following.

Arthur is told in a blue dream
Not to fight his stepson Mordred
The first time they meet in the field.
For, if they bloodily cross swords,
Arthur will surely perish neath
Mordred's stridently strong weapon,
Forever suff'ring blackened blame,
Losing Camelot.

Arthur, remembering Merlin,
Still pursuing chivalric peace,
Sends envoys to negotiate
With his declared damned enemy,
The sweat-soaked, hard-hearted, two-tongued Mordred.

Arthur watches battle begin.
While peace is parlayed, morsels munched,
A sloping, slithered adder bites
One of Mordred's murdering men
On his strengthened sinewed shoulder.
His sword is drawn to kill the snake
But sunlight sparkles off the blade,
Confusing the day.

Arthur, and others for and against,
Mistake quick cure for waging war.
Arthur's men draw several swords
To fight the clamouring claimant
Of the corrupt kingdom of Camelot.

Arthur and his men stand their ground
And hurl themselves into battle
Early in morning's guilty sun.
Valiant knights and square-hearted squires
Are armed to inflict mortal wounds
On the coarse combatting cowards
Through morn and into afternoon
'Til gloomy gloaming.

Arthur, his sharp vision failing
In the flailing, flashing flummox,
Drops Excalibur and scabbard,
Shining weapon and fond keeper
Of his fading life.

Arthur sees his dark-haired bastard
But does not flinch or stand away.
He snatches a spear from the corpse
Of a perished bloodied ally
And, head on, charges at Mordred,
Who, raising his demonic sword,
Crashes toward good King Arthur.
Now their ends are near.

Arthur drives his avenging spear
Into the rebel's restless heart.
Mordred's wicked weapon smashes
Into King Arthur's heav'nly head,
Both falling on to the offal-strewn ground.

Arthur calls to men still standing
To cast treasured Excalibur
And scabbard into the deep lake
Whence, years before, he had plucked them
From the fair hand of Ninianne.
But before any man can move,
Three silvery fairy queens rise
From a fragrant fog.

Arthur is lifted to a barge
The silvery sirens sail him
Away to Avalon to cure
The head-wounded king's hammered heart.
Mordred is left, dead, alone, abandoned.

Good King Arthur and Mordred fought
At the great Battle of Camlann.
That was the end of Camelot.

"That was," sings Aneirin, the Ollamh, "the Song of the End of Camelot. Aneirin sang it."

Notes

1. Little is known about Aneirin. What we do know is that he existed and functioned as a bard or poet in the courts of the warrior kings in the second half of the sixth century. We know, above all, that he wrote *The Gododdin*, the elegiac poem for a band of 600 warriors of the Gododdin region who fell in battle against the Saxons. It is the earliest known major work of literature in the western world and it was written or composed – never being intended to be written down – in Brythonic, an early form of the Welsh language. Aneirin, like his contemporary Taliesin, was said to have spent much of his time in the old north, the name that was then given to several of the kingdoms of post-Roman Britain.

   from "Aneirin and Taliesin: poets of the old North", by Phil Carradice
   http://www.bbc.co.uk/blogs/wales/entries/179daa23 -8adf-3c10-93b8-bb597ed30278

2. *The Gododdin* contains the first written reference to King Arthur:
   "He fed black ravens on the wall
   Of the fortress, although he was not Arthur."

3. Arthur was killed at the Battle of Camlann, 542AD.

Where do we go from here?

"Hungry?" she says.

"Nah," he drawls. "Not really." He lets out a lazy, lingering yawn.

"I've picked this fruit from the garden," she says. "I want you to taste it, to see what it's like. I think it's the best we've ever had."

"Later... later," he says. "Come here. It's too hot to do anything like hard work. In this heat, eating is hard work."

She lays down the fruit and comes over to him. They sprawl on the succulent grass.

"Isn't this great!" he says. "Nothing to do but enjoy the afternoon. Do you know, I think afternoon is my favourite time of day. We've done our work and now the rest of the day is ours. Laying here in the sun, seeing the plants grow, watching the animals, listening to the birds. Look at the sun! Not a cloud in the sky. Can you see any clouds?"

"No, darling," she murmurs, staring at his bronzing body. "I can't see any."

"D'y'know, I can't believe how lucky we are. Just you and me, pussy cat. No-one here to bother us. Just you and me in our own world. Paradise on earth."

She smooths her hand over his chest. "You are so beautiful," she says. "I adore your chest. Where did you get a chest like that? You've really caught the sun." Her hands move over him, gently feeling her way over his torso. "I've never seen a chest like this anywhere."

"Well, that's true," he laughs with delight. "And what's more, you'll never see another like it anywhere else!"

She grabs his thighs. "And legs, what legs. So firm, so muscular, so strong. Like a big brown bear."

He sits up, shifting his legs apart to keep balance and remain upright, inspecting her hands as they hold on to his thighs. "Well, they're all right. I've never really noticed my legs. To me, they're just hairy limbs that let me walk and run and climb trees and do the stuff legs are supposed to do."

"Oh no," she says. "They're more than that. They're part of what makes you so handsome. I love your legs. Your beautiful, beautiful... legs. Who'd've thought legs could be so bewitchingly beautiful. They can take us anywhere we want to go." She runs her hands down towards his feet, bends over and lightly kisses each knee. She peers up at him, giggling.

He falls back, also laughing, his legs splaying out almost at right angles to each other. As a sigh comes from the depths of his spirit, he closes his eyes and wraps an arm around her as she, too, closes her eyes.

They remain still, in union, as they bathe in the bright yellow sun, on the featherlight-grass, under the drowsingly cobalt sky, within the luscious warm breeze.

After a few minutes of lazy idling, she sits upright, looking about her, as if she has heard something.

From the near distance, a green and purple bird flaps and squawks its way towards them, hovers and then glides and lands a few feet away. It stands, staring at them, head cocked to one side.

"Oh!" she squeals, clapping her hands. "It's a – it's – what do you call it?"

He rouses himself up and rests back on his elbows. "Oh, that. I call it a parakeet."

"What a pretty name for a pretty creature." She mouths the word slowly to herself, as if hearing it for the first time. "Come here, pretty parakeet."

The parakeet creeps forwards and, as she leans over to stroke it, it opens its wings and flies upwards, away into the sky.

"It goes so high," she murmurs. "How does it get so high? Shall we ever get so high?"

"Why do you want to – I mean, we're happy here, aren't we? Come here, my little guinea pig."

But she is not satisfied. "It must be so wonderful to be able to get so high – to go so far away. All we ever do is stay here."

"Here is fine. Here is good. Here is where we are. Come here. Give me your arms."

She shakes her head with a violence she never knew she had – and which, for the first time in his life, shocks him. "Ha! Here is where we always are," she says, pouting. "Never there. Why can't we be there? Just once. Just for once, I want to be there. To see what it's like. That's all I ask. I mean, tell me, is that too much to ask?"

"Oh, my turtle dove, come here" he urges. "We're happy here, aren't we? You've always said you like it here. Let's be happy with where we are."

He lies back, his sun-burnished body inviting her enrapture, his black hair falling back to open his face out into the blazing heat. She turns to take in his hair-covered body.

But her meditation is interrupted by more flapping and squawking in the sky. She looks up to see, now, two parakeets flying through the air, side by side, opal green wings outstretched, flying so close to each other they are as one with one mind. Their pale green heads turn to see each other and, as they do so, they let out a unison echoing cry of such intimacy that it possesses the blueness of the air around, above and below them.

"Ooh!" she cries out. "Do you see that?"

But he sees nothing. His eyes are closed. "What?"

"See the – what are they?"

"Para – "

" – keet – I remember now. Para – "

" – keet," he finishes, still not opening his eyes.

"Parakeet, parakeet, parakeet, parakeet… What a pretty name for a pretty bird," she burbles, bouncing up and down with the joy of a new discovery. "Parakeet, parakeet, I love parakeet."

She rests back as she watches the two birds playing in the breeze, snuggling up to each other, then drawing away only to enjoy coming together again. Then, suddenly, one of them circles the other several times before disappearing into the distance, the other following until they are out of sight, as if they have never existed.

"Oh," she says, shedding a tiny tear. "They've gone... oh," – and she frumps back, the excitement over. She picks at the grass. "Don't you wish we were like that?"

"Like what?"

"The birds. Then we could fly away, like them, leave here and go and find new places... and do new things."

His eyes are still closed. "We're all right here."

"Even so," she says. "I mean, can't we just once be somewhere else, go somewhere else, like those – those – "

"Parakeets."

She nods hurriedly before she forgets. "Yes, of course. Silly me. Parakeets."

"We're all right here."

She looks him over. "I'm beautiful, aren't I? You do think I'm beautiful, don't you?"

He opens his eyes and stretches out his hand to stroke her flowing yellow hair. "Yes, my little piglet, you are very beautiful."

"And," she adds, "you do love me, don't you? Say you love me."

"You know I do."

She turns away and is startled to see the fruit, as if it has miraculously appeared from nowhere. She picks it up.

"I picked this fruit from the garden. I want you to taste it, to see what it's like. It's the best we've ever had."

He sits up and adjusts his body to sit cross-legged. "All right, then, give it here, let's have a look."

She holds out the fruit. "It's the best we've ever had."

He reaches out and takes it. He brings it slowly towards his face. "I don't remember seeing this before." He sinks his teeth into it, takes a mouthful, chews it around. "Mmm, not bad." He chews. He swallows.

His brain empties. His throat vibrates. His chest shakes. His groin quivers. His legs and feet tremble. He tries to keep balance. But his soul goes down, down his throat, through his body, down and through and down... and down. Rivulets of sweat cascade over him. And then, just as instantly, he shivers, and comes to. He looks down and lets out a screeching groan. He stands up, frightened, not knowing where to put his hands – but now and forever and always knowing exactly where to put his hands.

"Aah!" he screams. He looks about him, like a doomed victim, a hunted rabbit fearful for its life. "Oh, my fragrant tempting angel, what have you done?" He draws himself up, his eyes flitting everywhere, searching for hungry wolves. "We have to go."

"Go? I don't want to go. I like it here."

"Oh no, no, no, no, no!" he shouts. "You wanted to go. Well, you get your wish. We've got to go or we'll get caught – "

"Caught? What – "

"Can't you see? Look at us. I mean, look at us! Get up. Get up!" He pulls her up. "Leave the fruit. Put it down. Do as I tell you, can't you. Don't touch it. We have to go."

As she looks down to see the fruit roll away, her right arm covers her breasts, her left moves to hide her groin. She stares up at him. They stand, unable to move. They turn away, not knowing which way to go, not knowing what to do, realising they no longer have anything to say to each other. She bows her head as tears flow silently, uncontrollably.

"Oh, Adam," she whispers. "Where do we go from here?"

He shakes his head, lost, bewildered, broken. "God only knows."

Oedipus, carrier of lost truths

Sing, O Kalliopic Muse, of that awful truth that descends
That darkness-inspiring day, when the kind but rutheless
King Oedipus
Calls the old, blind, male and twice-sexed soothsayer to
narrate
The manner and the cause of the plague that besets his
failing rule.
Sing, O Cassandric Muse, in wondrous, misbegotten,
misheard voice
Of the wretched tale that besmirches our noble Theban
city;
As when, she foretells the decline of Priam's golden Troy,
Through the mountainous equine totem and the marauding
Greeks
Who counterfeit their way into that unprecedented polis
To monumental effect: she foretold the death of Patroklos,
The grief of noble, haughty, conquering Achilleus; the
decay
Of the love of Troylus and Criseyde, the mindless beauty
Of poor Helen; the end of decadal warring. So does she
sing.
Oedipus stands in silent disbelief when hearing the curse:
He will murder his good father, the upright Polybus,
Whose accursèd daughter Alcinoë will drown herself,
And marry his mother, Merope. Fearing for their lives,
Unable to countenance such fateful destiny, he flees
Corinth, departing Peloponnesia, his homeland.
He wanders he knows not where. Travelling towards his
accursèd
Blinding end, a three-way diversion, he encounters the
moment
Of his life, the point on which the world turns: a face-lined
old man.
O tragic cruciversing pathway! O fatal peripeteia!
This irrevocable Davlia from which there is no return!

Turn back, Oedipus, turn back, I say. Know that
Your precipitate actions lead to events reaching further
than you know.
But you do not hear the distant voice of future weeping
eyes,
You engage in childish, brutish querulousness;
You disrespect the wisdom of the confronting traveller;
Your defiant arrogance gives not an aged man his rightful
way;
Your youthful assumption of unseemly precedence
Dooms a traveller, kills a king, seals your diseasèd end.
Oedipus approaches the gates of Thebes, his unknown
home.
Shesepankh bars his way. She stands before him,
This Phix, this demi-woman demi-lion, guarding Thebes,
Their king Laius soon before killed by the unknown hand;
As the thrice capital Cerberus, mighty hellhound, guards
The living land of the dead, the gone, the ghosts, the
shades,
Against all who would flee that dreadful place. Who dares
To battle against progeny of monstrous Gaia-borne
Typhon
And deadly serpentine Echidna? So does she guard.
But she is no equal for the proud, swollen-footed hero,
Whose tale of Man's thrice pedestrianism supersedes;
This careful, exhausted creature throws herself to death;
He frees the city to cheerful resounding hallelujahs,
And claims his prize: beautiful, limpid Queen Jocasta,
Antigone, Ismene, Eteocles, Polynices are their offspring;
Laius' destroyer wanders the land freely; a plague
descends
On Thebes and will remain 'til the regicidal culprit is
found.
It is to Oedipus Rex, solver of riddles defiant of Fate,
That the Thebans turn to rescue them from this bottomless
depth
And deliver them from this evil-sodden existence;
As when, Akhenaten, wise leader of Aegyptic peoples,

Befuddled and surrounded by hieratic deities,
Clears his temples of polytheistic idols clouding
His races, and so leads them to monodeist clearness,
Cleansed, forward-looking. So does Oedipus intend to
lead.
He calls upon the unwilling prophet of the soul to aid the
search.
Oh, Wise One, saith he from his lofty throne-height
Down upon the bent-backed, stick-supported sage,
We are riven by this widespread plague, this addle-riddled
rot.
We are cursèd, the gods look on us with disfavour.
What have we done but failed to find the fellsman of our
erstwhile king?
Name this man, Old Man, and whosoever it be,
Friend or enemy, neighbour or brother, warrior or lover,
We will pluck out his eyes, we will break his soul,
We will condemn him to wander this earth as a beggarly
mite
With nothing but his grave, most grave, sins to accompany
him.
Sire, saith the nil-sighted pensioner, I beg with thee
That thou desisteth. Appease the gods in other ways;
Pursueth not the folly of discovery.
Thou art mad, Tiresias, screams Oedipus;
This is the way, this is the truth. Whoever it may be,
He is condemned. 'Tis thee, Old Man, who lacks foresight,
Who holds the blame. I accuse thee, Tiresias,
Of all that thou knowest but will not tell.
Tiresias draws himself up, his crooked aging back
No more of old age and as straight as his tree-hewn stick,
His height double his previous self; as when, mighty Zeus
Elevated over Cronus to compel him to disgorge
His siblings swallowèd out of jealous fearfulness;
As those sired by Hera, Poseidon, Hades, Demeter, Rhea,
Hestia
Were freed by o'ertowering Zeus. So does Tiresias stand.
He unfurls the mysteries of Delphic prophecies;

Of how Laius and Jocasta fear for their son, Oedipus,
After the prophecy that he will kill his father
And marry his mother; and, so, mountainside, they
abandon him;
So Oedipus is found, raised by Polybus and Merope
As their own; so he learns of the prophecy that he kills
His father and marries his mother. So he flees from their
care.
So he meets his father, Laius, and kills him. So he meets
the Sphinx.
So he frees Thebes. So he marries his mother, Jocasta.
O great king, saith Tiresias, thou hast done great things,
Thou hast liberated this great city from ransom and ill,
And in doing, envelopèd it in thine own ransom and ill.
Thus thou art thine own beginning, middle and thine own
ending.
Jocasta falls down on the dust-strewn sun-beaten ground,
Her children recoil in horror from this poison-laden queen,
Products of her incest with their father who is their
brother.
O my king, my husband, my son, my patricidal partner,
What demons hast thou releasèd into the venal air,
What hast thou done! Dare not to cast your eyes on me
again!
So saying, she leaves his side, her eyes shrouded over,
Her wailing drowning out sorry songbirds, chirping
crickets,
She finds herself a room, hugger-mugger, and knots a
deathly rope,
Able to live no more with her own besmirchèd soul,
A bedraggled spirit, of this world no more, she pays
Kharon, the ruffian ferryman, to cross the Styx and be with
Shades.
'Tis insufficient. For Oedipus loved her in ignorance
Of previous concegenated blood. He found her drooping
flesh,
Her limp body still clothed; her beauteous brooch,
Which he takes and, facing nothingness for ever more,

Pierces his eyes 'til blinded from the base of his soul
To the uppermost hairs on the top of his head.
His pain complete; his release divine-driven; his lesson
learned;
As Tiresias foretold, Oedipus wanders the earth for ever
more,
Warning others that the gods cannot be defied, must not
be.
Proclaim, O Ananke, that it is a cruel truth to be told
By the gods we are powerless to transport ourselves nearer
To the gods; that we are powerless in this life, and the
next;
And an even crueller truth to travel the aimless road to
Thebes
Not knowing that this truth will always be; only to find
At the shameful eye-gorging end, that the only thing we
know is
We know nothing; we knew nothing: and that is all we will
ever know.

How It Happened

1. I shift Alpha Centauri. I create the Virgo Cluster.
2. A spontaneous amusement in My mind forms Black Holes.
3. A formless star is born without My permission. I destroy it.
4. I determine the existence of hydrogen atoms.

   – Lord, you summon me.
   – Michael, Lucifer lets himself be proud and so is not pleased with his place in the Angelic Hierarchy. He will try to enlist your support for his cause.
   – My Lord.
   – He will tell you that, without you, he has a lost cause. You will tell him that, while you cannot support him, he should proceed as he has a just cause.
   – What reason shall I give for not supporting him?
   – Tell him, Michael, that I am in your soul and you are powerless to raise arms against your own soul. Go now and wait for him to approach you.
   – My Lord.

5. I create Earth, My Special Place where all bow before Me.
6. I point My finger at Earth and Adam, whose name means Man, is born. Eve, the Living One, breathes by his side.
7. I allow My name to be known as Zeus, Zoroaster, Huitzilopochtli, Inti, Huang Tian Shang Di, Yahweh, Pitjantjatatjara.
8. In the twinkling of Mine eye and as I have pre-ordained, my Only Begotten Son is crucified.

- Lucifer whispers, Will you join me, Michael?
- Michael says, You will face permanent exile from Heaven, whose name means Where God Dwells, and also Sky and Firmament.
- I hear Lucifer say, I know that I am right.
- Michael says, Our Lord is with us. If He says you are right, you do not need me. Our Lord is the Truth. You will be victorious without me.
- Lucifer says, I will raise an army and I will be Master of all I survey.
- I let seep into his soul that, of that and that alone, he is right.

9. Socrates dies. Shakespeare is born.
10. I give life to Planet UB313 in Star Cluster M4, Constellation Scorpius.
11. I allow Man the discovery of the philosophy of Gravity.
12. Man, in his insect-like ambition, leaves his home planet to bestride his Moon.
13. The Earth Star dies.
14. While the Angels clamour and fight, I create a place in Heaven for Michael and the victors to rest. I do not interfere as I have decided the outcome.
15. Lucifer will be defeated to demonstrate that, while Free Will belongs to all, My given privilege of making wrong decisions results in pre-destined Doom.
16. Minor explosions in 59,902 galaxies at the far end of My consciousness cause Me insignificant concern. I become impatient with 3,900,000,000,000 squabbling stars in Galaxy z8 GND 5296.
17. Alpha Centauri shifts in the wake of the death of the Earth Star.
18. I impose My will upon all I have created and wipe everything away.
19. I start again.

This is the name of the leader of the Heavenly Rebellion: Lucifer, whose name means Bringer of Light, and who is now named Satan, which means Adversary and Accuser.

These are the names of My Personal Warriors who went against Me:

— Asmodeus, who becomes the demon of lust and twisted sexual desires;
— Sammael, who is the angel of death;
— Lilith, whose name means night creature, night monster, night hag, screech owl;
— Ahriman, whom I created to oppose Me;
— Balan, with serpent's tail, eyes that shoot fire, heads of bull, man and ram;
— Baliel, whose name means worthless;
— Molloch, who demands child sacrifices.

And these are the names of the Angels who defied me:

— Samyaza, Arstikapha, Armen, Kakabael, Turel, Rumyel, Danyal, Kael, Barakel, Azazel, Armers, Bataryal, Basasael, Ananel, Turyal, Simapiseel, Yetarel, Tumael, Tarel, Rumel, Azazyel.

20. In a distant dimension, I create a place for the Fallen Angels to nurse their sorry wounds and miserable pride. I name it Hell, which means Nether World Of The Dead and One Who Covers Up Or Hides.
21. I despatch them to That Place, from which there is no return or escape.
22. For now it is known, and forever and always, that I am all-Knowing, all-Powerful, all-Being.
23. I am Three in One, World without Beginning, World without End, World without Time.

Lightning Source UK Ltd.
Milton Keynes UK
UKOW04f1923180917
309425UK00001B/148/P